The Road to Redemption

A Journey from Despair to Happiness

by

Beverly Davis

Scripture quotations are taken from the New International, King James, Easy Read, and New American Standard versions of the Bible.

Edited 2024

Disclaimer

This book is a Christian fiction work. Any names, situations, or similarities in the circumstances are purely coincidental and do not reflect real-life characters. They are included solely to depict possible situations to apply biblical principles.

The spiritual principles and scriptural lessons outlined in this story are for real-life applications.

Cover Design by Beverly Davis

DEDICATION

Dedicated to my mother who sacrificed everything for us.

Marion Brown

Preface

My life's journey prompted me to question the concept of love and its true meaning. I decided to do some research on love, its meaning, and how to recognize it in yourself and in others who claim to love you. More importantly, I wondered about the feelings and emotions that most people identify as love, which are not love at all. I chronicled my research, which was quite long and tedious to anyone who was not on my path and stored it away. The study detailed the power of attraction, the joy that affection for someone brings, the deep emotions that lust invokes, and the human brain's response to those things. Finally, I researched what the scripture says about love, which is where I should have started.

Over the years, I have listened to heartbreaking stories from women who are in desperate situations. By the time I talk to them, they have already loved and lost someone who declared their love for them. After they traveled down the "love" road together, one or the other found themselves with a wrecked life and a broken heart. So, what happened? They started with hope and passionate feelings for each other that I can now put in the category of infatuation. When the passion wears off, as it inevitably does, and the intense feelings fade, they find themselves with someone that they sometimes do not want at all.

Some studies show that infatuation lasts from three to five years; other research says a much shorter period. In either case, this is the period when we see our mates as wonderful, kind, perfect, and the best thing that ever happened to us. Perhaps in the infatuation stage, we need to exercise the most caution. We are in the "love cloud" and more likely to make poor decisions if we make those decisions based on our emotions.

Many people change themselves and rearrange their lives to suit the person they love. They compromise the moral and ethical guidelines they set for themselves and make great sacrifices only to find themselves stuck and left shedding tears with their hearts broken. So many of them don't recognize that the person they are involved with has hidden agendas. Neither do they know how to distinguish love from lust, infatuation, or just plain selfishness. My role, in many cases, is to help the injured party pick up the pieces of their lives to start again after the love experience is over. I hope this book will serve to open someone's eyes before their lives suffer damage and brokenness, or that it helps them recover from their error in judgment.

The inspiration to write "The Road to Redemption" has three aspects: stories that I've heard, my own life's lessons, and my desire to understand, fully, our inner motivations to pick and stay with someone unsuitable for us. What makes us unable to see, clearly, our intended's motives? My life's story required that I understand what love really is and how to recognize it. I believe that many others also need this information.

"The Road to Redemption" is a story of the redemptive power of God. He stands ready to forgive and guide us to a new place of peace. The God who watches over the universe watches over us. He understands our journey better than we do and can use our misfortunate blind spots, established throughout our lives, to strengthen us. His strength can perfect us when we are weak.

The Road to Redemption chronicles the life of Janice Burns, her early life influences, and the experiences that shaped her view of love. She faces profound failure and rebounds to a successful life and future. This fictional character is a compilation of many women and their stories. It begins with a picture of my childhood, which was a painful memory for me, and made it a challenge to write. Each chapter has a principle tied to a verse from the Bible.

I wrote this book for any woman who finds herself in the crosshairs of a relationship that is good to her, but bad for her. There is a fine line between lust and love. This story will uncover the realization that we can have scotomas, or places in our field of understanding and vision, that render us unable to see what is clear to an outsider watching our actions. According to Lou Tice of the Pacific Institute, "We develop these blind spots by holding erroneous information from negative experiences in our lives deep in our subconscious minds that keep us from distinguishing the actual truth from the residuals of our negative experiences. Because it is internal information, we respond to situations on autopilot, without consciously realizing that we are acting based on previous personal experiences."

This story will bring light and understanding. "The Road to Redemption" is a journey to God. God is love. It also serves as a guide to help anyone find their way out of a failure in life that they feel they cannot overcome. An absolute collapse in judgment can be devastating, but the road back to respectability can be, and is, a path back to God.

Prologue

Janice was having her usual morning coffee admiring the magnificent beauty of the sunrise early Sunday morning. Her husband was sleeping in the next room, and her daughters were getting their last moments of sleep before she would have to wake them up for breakfast. Janice enjoyed her peaceful, quiet time before her husband and children woke up. She enjoyed these moments because they gave her time to reflect on life and make a schedule for her day before the rush of a family morning began.

Her life was splendid, with a successful career as a Physician's Assistant and a beautiful family; Janice was truly happy. She had worked hard and accomplished all the visions and goals that she made for herself. Her marriage was secure, and they were amazingly compatible and content. Together they were able to have a successful marriage, careers, and reasonably happy children. She picked up her phone and began scrolling through her friend's posts when she saw a post that caused her to pause and read. The post was exceptionally long, and usually, Janice would have passed it over, but this morning, she was relaxed and had the time to read.

While she read the post, she could visualize the scene as it unfolded before her. The police had pulled a young girl over onto a side street for a traffic violation. The girl, still in her pajamas, disheveled and obviously upset, stopped her car, jumped out, and stood to wait for the officer to approach her. Her three young children in the car were still in their pajamas and without proper restraints. The officer walked up and requested her license and registration. People came out onto their porches to watch the spectacle, half of them were concerned for the children, and the others were just curious.

As the officer explained why she stopped her, the young woman began to blurt out her explanation. Her words came tumbling out without censors. Her live-in fiancé` attacked her, so she took her children and fled the house to avoid further confrontation. He threatened her, and she believed that she and her children were in danger. The house belonged to her, and she allowed him to move in recently. He was still there, and when she ran out of the house, she left her purse with her driver's license inside. In her haste to get to safety, she also failed to put the children into seatbelts.

As the police officer looked at her with a mixture of pity and irritation, the girl must have realized that she was digging a hole for her young beau as the officer's questions began to center more on him than on her. She was now asking about his actions. "Had he hit the children, had he hit her?" The girl switched to explaining what he did, justifying his actions. The police officer explained to her that she would have to give her a ticket, but she felt that it was not safe for her to return home. The girl protested, saying she thought it would be okay now. He just needed some time to calm down. The officer, almost pleading, said these words to her, "He is telling you who he is; believe him."

How often do we tolerate unacceptable behavior from the ones who profess to love us, then justify, defend, and explain it away as this girl did? We rationalize bad choices made all "in the name of love" that eventually lead us into an unmanageable life.

The officer gave her the best advice she could, "Believe what you see." This girl hoped for a different outcome than her undeniable reality was screaming for her to consider. She felt unsafe enough to take her children and run, but now she was downplaying her boyfriend's actions. According to the officer, "The person she left at her home was exactly who his actions said he was." Janice wondered what had brought this girl to this point, and what would have to happen to resolve the situation. Would she make the necessary changes to protect the future of herself and her children? Would she continue in her current situation, hoping for a different outcome other than what was actually the truth about her life now? At that moment, Janice's mind drifted to her own life. She thought about how easily the post she had just read could have been her story instead of the life she experienced.

Janice understood that we are all born into circumstances that are out of our control, and just as we cannot control the circumstances of our birth, we are helpless to control many of the events we encounter as children. We can, however, as adults, through the power of God, see the truth and let the Holy Spirit empower us to make the changes that will bring lasting peace to our lives.

Janice's life started with ideal conditions that slowly disintegrated into an existence that reshaped her ideas and emotional world. As she grew and matured, her circumstances and realities developed her idealistic points of view into biased and unrealistic ideals.

After closing the posts that morning, Janice walked into the room and looked at her beautiful 12 and 14-year-old daughters as they slept. Almost instinctively, she decided to write her story for them. Janice decided to catalog and chronicle her lessons and tell them about God's redeeming grace that she encountered along the way. She would start with her early life, which set the stage for her inability to truthfully interpret and adequately respond to situations that would confront her.

The effects of Janice's lack of control over her circumstances as a child later surfaced and caused her to create a reality from which she felt she needed to escape. She would tell her daughters the story of a girl who allowed her emotions to over-rule her better judgment. She made life-affecting changes based on someone else's selfish desire for her.

During her formative years, Janice visualized a future where she would have a career, a husband, and children. They would live in a beautiful home, happily ever after. She was not conscious of the fact that she was mentally creating her future family using a broken model acquired when she was a child in her own family. She was also unaware that along with the family prototype she had built in, there was also a built-in one for a husband like her father, a professional, well-dressed, handsome man who was physically present but emotionally out of sync with his family. Her dad provided her with a picture of the ideal husband. She still loved him and always longed for his love in return. The boys she found attractive would fit into the image of the father who abandoned her.

She would also tell her daughters the story of the redemptive power of God that had embraced her. He took the negative in her life and brought about positive results. Her story is one of hope that chronicles her profound failure and her path to recovering from that failure. The story would tell of the courage it took to push forward, forgive herself, and rebuild her life.

CONTENTS

Preface

Prologue

ACKNOWLEDGMENTS

Keisha Davis for her inspiration

Chapter 1
Values

The LORD will keep you from all harm—he will watch over your life.
Psalm 121:7

Our sense of self-worth is often formed using our early life experiences and impressions that we often cannot control. We internalize those experiences, and they influence us in at least two ways: the way we govern our lives and our decision-making process. They serve as the basis for what we will and will not allow in our lives. If you have ever wondered why you think the way you do, chapter one will help you uncover the mystery.

Early Life

Charles and Maria Burns met when they were only teenagers. Introduced by a mutual friend, they soon became inseparable. They attended every school event together. Their high school senior class crowned them "Most Devoted Couple" in their school yearbook. Charles attended the local college and majored in Engineering. The two continued to date, and after his graduation, they married. Charles focused on his career and spent most of his time off away from home, working, networking, and trying to meet people who could help him advance in his career. Maria, on the other hand, was a homemaker and nest-builder. Everyone knew this marriage would last forever because they were so much in love and only had eyes for each other. They had a small wedding with only their families in attendance as they began their lives together as husband and wife. They were a perfect match, or so it seemed. Only after their third child, Janice, was born did the ideal marriage begin to show signs of deterioration.

Janice's earliest memories were of a happy, carefree

childhood. She attended a neighborhood school that was very close to her home. She recalled the first day of school as always being exciting. There were pretty new clothes and shoes to start the new school year. Her mother had the habit of dressing Janice and her sister alike, their outfits identical except for the colors. Janice loved new clothes, and she enjoyed dressing like her older sister. Somehow, it made her feel a little more grown-up. Her mother would cook a big breakfast every morning, and the aroma would be a silent call to the table to start each day.

Then there was the excitement of meeting the new teacher and many new classmates. Yes, the first day of class was her favorite day. Classwork was always easy for her. She looked forward to her daily morning walk, and as she strolled along with her older brother and sister, they passed familiar houses and enjoyed small commentaries on who lived there or the flower gardens. She would encounter her neighborhood friends along the way, and some of them would wait on their porches until she reached their homes. Then they would join in, and they would all walk to school together. Janice felt well-liked and made friends with ease at school.

Being the middle child of her family created several dynamics with which Janice had to learn to cope. According to Lynn Griffin in her article "The Secret Power of Middle Children," middle children are falsely considered to be neglected, resentful, have a negative outlook, and feel like they do not belong. They have many strengths, trust in friendships, and work harder to overcome people's negative preconceived notions of them. Middle children are loyal, great negotiators, and great team leaders. Because of their lack of attention at home, Griffin says, this can be a positive, as they do not have huge egos. They dislike conflict and avoid addressing problems in marriage or at work. They are less likely to stray in relationships, and because of their family position and having to wait, they are also patient." This profile fits Janice almost perfectly.

Janice loved her family, but being a well-adjusted child in her family was a lot like being invisible. She did not have the distinction of being the oldest child, nor the youngest, not the tallest, nor the shortest, not anything special about her that would bring attention her way. Her oldest brother was the first in the family to do many things, while her sister was academically brilliant. Her younger brother was the baby, which alone made him unique, but Janice was just okay. She was well-balanced and happy, but she also remembered when she was the baby of the family with all its exclusive privileges. The older children got special rights and permissions because of their age, while her younger brother assumed her youngest child status and with it, the rewards of being the baby. She missed being the one her mother fussed over and their time spent together after the older children went to school. That kind of time with Mom now belonged to the brother, who was the youngest of the family. Janice discovered early that at school, she could be unique, not just one person in a large group. After school, she loved to play with her classmates who lived near her. There were lively baseball games and jacks on the front porch where she boasted about being an expert.

Friday was allowance day. Her grandfather would come on Friday with a big bag of treats; she especially loved the fruit and donuts he would bring. All the kids would gather around to see what he had in his armload of pastries; sometimes, he would even bake a cake. Granddad was an expert baker. Next, he would reach into his pocket and pull out everyone's allowance for the week. After school, in anticipation of their grandfather's arrival, they discussed how they would spend their allowance that evening because the neighborhood store always had toys on sale. Days playing games after school would be even more pleasant when she saved money from her allowance to go to the neighborhood store to buy cookies and candy for snacks. Her granddad would return on Sunday to take everyone to Sunday school and church. He was a church officer and devout believer.

Janice's father was a handsome engineer who spent long hours at the office. Always impeccably dressed, he bought a beautiful new car every other year. She loved him dearly. He was her hero. It was not that he ever paid much attention to her, but when he came in from work, the house would light up with activity and chatter. When she was younger, and he would come in from work, she would run to him and grab his legs, lifting herself from the floor to ride the rest of the way down the hall on his leg. It would make him smile, and she loved that.

She never thought that his lack of attentiveness towards her was her fault; after all, he had a lot to think about with his job and providing for such a large family. Once he settled himself at home, there would be a family dinner, and then he would disappear into his bedroom or leave the house. His emotional disconnection was not only towards her; he was emotionally distant from everyone in the house. It was just his way, a part of his personality, and for their household, it was normal. There were moments of affection, but they disappeared as quickly as they appeared.

They always ate dinner as a family with everyone at the table, and she was delighted when he was there. At the dinner table, they all chattered about school and neighborhood happenings. However, her father was old-fashioned and felt that children should know their places and stay in them. It was always important to behave well, display proper table manners, and request permission to leave the table after they completed their meal. They were required to wait for an okay from one or the other of her parents before they left the table. It was a must in their home to compliment their mother on the meal she had prepared. Janice thought it was silly because she did not always enjoy the meal, but he said that they had to appreciate the time their mother spent preparing those meals.

Their television was in the family room of their home. They only had one, and they all watched the same programs together. Their mother insisted on some cultural programs, which they all hated, probably so that she could endure the other programs that they liked. This was the tone of family life for Janice, and it was a stable, loving, caring environment.

Maria Burns enjoyed staying at home and taking care of the family. She adored her children and took great pride in caring for them. Her Sunday morning ritual was to read the comics to them at breakfast. Maria would listen to the radio a lot. She was easygoing, loving, and extremely beautiful. She would play the piano for the children and show them dances from her teen years. That was always a lot of fun. Her mother was an avid storyteller, and at night, they would sit in a circle around her and intently listen while she wove the most exciting and sometimes even scary stories. Her eyes would get large, and she used her hands and gestured a lot to demonstrate one point or another.

They were a typical middle-class family who lived in a neighborhood with other middle-class families. They enjoyed birthday parties and swimming lessons, piano lessons, and trips to the beach. Her parents handled their disagreements out of the earshot of their children so that the children were never aware of any problems their parents might have. Their home was peaceful. Life was ideal; they lacked nothing. Janice had no idea that her perfect life was about to change.

Storybook Life to Nightmare

It all seemed to change so suddenly. One day life was terrific, and the next day, disaster. The day started as usual on Friday. As they dressed for school, they laughed and talked about how their grandparents' pet dog, Red, would be waiting for them when they got home. Her grandparents lived a block away, and Red would show up unprompted every Friday after school and stay the weekend before going back. They knew to sit on the porch and watch for him; without fail, he would come. After he stayed all weekend, as if he had an inner signal, he would leave on Sunday evening. When her younger brother started school, Red would walk him to school Monday morning and be waiting for him after school to walk him home. Then he would go back to her grandparent's house. His appearance was something they all looked forward to and enjoyed because they did not have a pet of their own. They joked about how the dog was part human.

This Friday would be different from any other, however. Her mom called them together to announce that their Dad had decided not to be a part of their family any longer. He was leaving, and they would no longer be able to stay in their middle-class home. The fact was, he was already gone and would not be returning. At nine years old, it was puzzling to her, but she would soon feel the full impact of his abandonment because life was about to take a turn for the worse. The family's income would severely decline, and they would move to a less than desirable neighborhood different from any she could even remember visiting.

Pregnant with her fifth child and abandoned, her mother became severely depressed to the point of breakdown. She struggled alone to figure out how to support her children and maintain their household. Janice now felt even more invisible than ever, and that ignored feeling would eventually deteriorate into feeling unloved. When feeling unnoticed and insignificant was added to all the changes in their lives, her self-esteem plummeted.

Janice arrived at her new home after dark one night. When she woke up that first morning in her new home for her first look at the neighborhood, she was unfamiliar with it and she did not like it. This apartment was incredibly smaller than the sprawling house with the large yard and front porch they had known so well. She ventured outside. It had rained the night before, and there were about four feet of water covering the street at the end of their block so that the roadway and curb were not visible. She walked toward it as far as she could without stepping into the water. What a curious thing; Janice had never experienced seeing a flooded street before. Floodwater covered several of the porches of the apartments in the neighborhood. It looked like a small river. She had never been anywhere like that before; what a strange place. Life the way she understood it had vanished, and her friends were gone, as was the school she loved. She found herself separated from the neighbors she knew so well and looked at the rows of tenement houses in the new neighborhood, which were cold and unfamiliar. They were all identical houses, all exactly alike, and she had to make a note of the number on the door to remember which one belonged to her. It was a strange place and an eerie feeling, and nothing was recognizable; nothing felt right. Her father was gone, her home was no more, the security of their home vanished, there was no way to go back, and she felt isolated, bewildered, and utterly lost.

The family's existence became simplified; they were not the worst off financially in their neighborhood, but certainly not the most comfortable. Their possessions were a shadow of where they came from; their Oriental rug on the living room floor, their furniture, and the porch furniture (theirs was the only porch that had furniture), were small things that hinted at a more prosperous life. Maria Burns was recovering from a nervous breakdown. She suffered the breakdown after her family separation, and she was oddly present and absent at the same time. In fact, she felt as helpless and as lost as her children did.

Things changed a lot after her Dad left his family, gone were the days when their neighbors were doctors and lawyers, and mothers did not work. In her new single-parent household, none of the amenities existed that they had before. There were no longer songs while her mother played the piano, no swimming lessons, or birthday celebrations. Her mother did not read the comics on Sunday mornings, and they no longer attended church. The truth was Janice spent a lot of time in those years being embarrassed about the lack of standard necessities her mother was unable to provide, and these days she only fantasized about having pretty clothes like the other girls at school. Everything that had been good in their lives just ended abruptly. There was less of everything, less food, fewer clothes, less love.

As their mother's life changed, so did her children's lives. With her breakdown behind her, she became the household provider. After her baby was born, she worked hard as a domestic. Her depression and exhaustion continued. Her beauty faded, and deep folds appeared on her face while she pushed forward with all the energy she could muster. These days the children were mostly on their own, trying to pick up the pieces of their lives with little guidance or support. Their grandparents were no longer a block away, so they rarely got to see them these days.

Somehow those years passed by, and they assimilated into their new environment. Janice made friends as quickly as she always had, and once she got past being the new girl at school, she actually felt okay about her new environment. They did not eat together anymore nor laugh together at the dinner table as they had in the past. If the truth is told, they rarely sat at the dinner table together except on holidays now. Everyone survived the best way he or she could. No one seemed happy, least of all Janice.

Knowledge is power. In their former lives, they attended Sunday school and church. Janice learned there that she could pray and ask God for what she desired for her future. Their mother taught them to pray every night before they went to bed. Now in her new life, she made it her ritual every night to talk to God about what she wanted her life to look like again. She prayed for her future home, family, education, the kind of job she would have, and the number of children she wanted. There was no obvious way these things could happen for her now, but she prayed for them anyway. "Well," she thought, "Isn't God the one who could change anything?" She believed she could have a wonderful life, and God was the one who would help her do it. That knowledge motivated her. She clung to everything she could learn about him. Yes, surely, He was the one who could restore sanity to her life. Jesus was the only thing she could keep from her former life; she held on to Him tightly.

Before now, Janice always loved the excitement of the first day of school. This time, starting a new school was an intimidating experience. Because the school year was already in progress, Janice's first day started with the School Principal escorting her to class. It was not at all like the school she left, a new, well-built school. This school was old and creepy. None of the faces she saw were familiar, and they all watched her as she slowly found her way to the seat that the teacher pointed out for her to take. The feeling of alienation she felt that day would stay with her for a long time. She did her best to blend in that first day, but the estrangement from

9

her former life only felt stronger as she struggled to find her place in this new setting.

As usual, it took her only a short time to make new friends and adapt to her new environment. Once she made friends at school, her elementary school days became as delightful as before. Her home life was still a struggle, but she created a world for herself to live in away from home. She survived as she always had at school while she became even more of a loner within her family. Janice's feeling of isolation within her family gradually transformed into a sense of being an outsider. Her only ally was the God that she prayed to at night; he always listened to how she felt.

Junior high school was a breeze, and Janice remained quite a dedicated scholar. Each year she became stronger and stronger emotionally and academically. There was rarely any word from her father now, and even though he never answered, she wrote to him occasionally to keep in touch. It helped to numb herself to his lack of response.

High School

At last, Janice was a high school senior, and she enjoyed every minute of it. School had always been her refuge, but after her father left, her time at school was more important than ever. Janice excelled academically and was very active in school activities. She especially enjoyed singing in the school chorus. Her strong singing voice led to her being chosen occasionally to sing lead parts and solos. She found refuge and peace in these activities and gave them all her energy. At school, she could pretend that life was okay. She was in a world she created and not captive in a world that she did not want and had no control over. At school, she was in complete control of her own life.

Life at home was still close to unbearable for her, and she

was despondent when she had to be there. The family had crumbled into a "survival of the fittest" camp. All of them slept in the same house, but the days of the chattering and laughing about anything were over. Her time at school was the only place where she could feel normal again. Her mother continued to recover from her depression, but she still was not the happy, home building, nurturing person they had once known. They saw less of their Grandfather, who had been their inspiration since they no longer lived a short walk from him. Granddad did not drive, and they were very far away from him. His loss meant there was no positive male role model anymore. There was no man to love them, support their hopes, no more allowances, no more Sunday morning taking them to church, no more...

Determined to make the best of her new circumstances, Janice got involved in the many community activities that were available around them. She joined all the clubs and teams offered by the many community groups who came into the area to help poor, disadvantaged people. Her affiliation with them helped her feel more like a part of the area where she now had to live. Her old friends and neighbors slowly faded from her memory, which made the sting of leaving her old home less sad for her. She still clung to the memories of her former house, though, with its large, spacious rooms, beautiful furnishings, and its large yard with pecan trees and wisteria. When she passed through beautiful neighborhoods, she always remembered how it felt to live there. Janice often wondered if she would ever live in a beautiful house again. It was one of her secret prayers when she talked to God at night, but she never shared her thoughts with anyone. It was just too embarrassing to let anyone know her inability to let go of her past. Her mother did all she could to keep them together, and Janice would not even whisper that it was not enough.

Janice focused her attention on her future with its limitless possibilities. She was closer than ever to being able to fulfill her desire to leave her current home. Wherever she went, she would be able to live on her own and create happiness for herself, just as she had in high school. Going away to college was the first step in her independence plan. She spent hours thinking about what it would be like to live on campus; she hoped it would be all that she imagined it to be. She read everything she could find about dormitory life over and over. She intently studied pictures of students living on college campuses. The images were so pretty, and the people in the ads looked happy. She imagined herself in those pictures, living in those rooms, studying, and meeting new friends. She just knew that when she got there, her experience would be great!

Her mother had hammered home the idea that education would provide the opportunity that could change her life forever. She insisted that if the chance to go to college had been hers, they would not be living in their current situation. Her mother said, "College would have prepared her for more profitable employment." She also said, "Because she could not further her education, they were forced to live in their current situation." She insisted that her children did not need to suffer such a fate. They could take hold of the opportunities that had eluded her. As it was, Janice's mother had to take the least in unskilled employment and work very hard for very little. It caused her to be exhausted and disheartened as the happy mother they once knew faded into an abyss.

As Janice looked for colleges, she also applied to take the SAT. She did not have much information to go on. No one else in her inner circle of friends was even interested in going to further their education at a higher learning institution. They all had their sights set on getting jobs, getting married, and starting families. Nevertheless, Janice had other ideas; she searched the Internet and looked at virtual images of campus after campus as she heard about new ones. She knew she would be happy with any one of those. She had never been more than forty-five minutes from home, so she sent her applications to schools that seemed far away. The truth was that none of them was more than one state away. Janice was not aware that her world had grown very small. She could hardly wait to start a new chapter in her life.

Janice was somewhat apprehensive about traveling so far away alone; there would be no advance trips with family to visit the campus. Nor would there be any family visits once she was gone. Her family's financial position would not allow them to do any of those things. There was no help for her with which college to pick. If she wanted to go, she had to do the research and find her way without help. This decision was hers without the aid of experienced adults. No, she was facing an unknown future, and she was facing it alone. It was exciting and frightening at the same time. Exciting, because she would have a place where she did not feel invisible or feel unloved, that idea was exhilarating. The thought of separating from what was currently familiar surroundings was frightening; it had become home, the norm. She feared it would be as it had been when she first moved here, locked out of her past and forced into a future full of unknowns. She pressed forward.

During her last year of school, she was able to get a job after school and began earning money for the things she needed for her senior class activities. It made her feel good to earn money, and hope started to surge in her heart. At 17 years old, she had to learn what sized clothes to buy. Up to that point, almost everything she wore came from boxes of thrift store clothes given to her family. She made the best of it and even learned to do her hair so well it looked professionally done. She became proficient at making it so that, outwardly, everything appeared to be going well. Before she got her job, she felt helpless, and now she felt things were changing for the better.

As graduation day came closer and closer, she carefully made her well-thought-out choice of a school in a nearby town, Johnson State University, and read a lot about it. It was in Clayton, North Carolina, a small town outside of Goldsboro. She aspired to be a Physician's Assistant, and they had an excellent program. Janice loved to care for people and enjoyed and excelled in her science classes. A career in which she could help people and do what she loved would suit her well. The school counselor had not given her any information, and since no one who lived around her had ever been to college or even wanted to go, they were all planning to get married; Janice was alone in her quest to find just the right school. Therefore, she chose as carefully as she could and used all the information she could gather. She pored over the list of what she needed and filled herself with images of being there. On days she got paid, Janice purchased items from the website the college published for freshmen students. One or two a payday, she was making progress in fulfilling the completion of listed items. Of course, since they did not have a car, travel to Johnson State would be made by bus. She calculated bus fares and the price of getting from the bus station to the school. She did not overlook any detail.

Frankly, she had no clue what to really expect from a life at college; all she knew was that in her current environment, she knew how to survive. She understood her surroundings and carried with her the remnants of a better life. As impaired as her family life was, it was familiar and offered a level of comfort. At least she knew what to expect. This move would take her out of her comfort zone more than she wanted to admit. Would she experience the same bewildering, lost feeling? It was an anxious thought, but there was no other escape route available.

Janice decided to be brave to face the future with courage. At last, she was old enough, and her hard work at school had empowered her to change her life completely. The moment she longed for finally arrived; it was her time. Everything was looking good; all of the details were working themselves out, her list of needs was getting smaller, and her acceptance to her prospective school was secured. Then she met Jason...

Reflective Questions

1. How could the blind spots Janice developed adjusting to her new world possibly cause her problems?

2. When there is no one to ask questions at home, where can you effectively look for help?

3. How would including God in your daily life help you succeed?

Prayer

Father, help me to be aware of my early life experiences that may cause me to stumble later. I surrender to the leading of the Holy Spirit, who leads me and guides me into all truth.

Chapter 2
Jason

Love is not selfish   **1 Corinthians 13:5**

We receive information in many ways. The Bible tells us to watch and pray. In hindsight, we often say, "I should have paid more attention." Paying more attention is what Janice should have done to keep her life plan on track. What are you ignoring or making rationalizations about that will affect your life later?

Janice Meets Jason

Janice is feeling good about her future. Her grades are excellent, and her job takes care of the things she needs that her mother just cannot afford. After choosing the best educational institution herself, and after what seems like a very long time, Jan feels optimistic about her life. It feels to her like beginning the process of waking up from a nightmare. Had it been that many years since their lives fell apart? At this point, it does not even matter. On track and mentally focused, the momentum of success and progress grows with every day that passes.

Janice met Jason Miller during her final year of high school. He was a popular boy who happened to be in her homeroom class. They had several classes together and sat next to each other in two of them. Soon after they met, they started having long conversations whenever they saw each other during their lunch hour at school. After the third conversation, they found themselves looking for each other and then planning when and where they would meet outside of the cafeteria so that they could find seats together more often. He was handsome and amusing; she liked how he could draw everyone's attention to him, joking around and giving advice on anything and everything. Some of his jokes were harsh and caused

Janice to cringe when he targeted someone to make fun of, but everyone laughed, and no one ever actually got angry. Janice thought he went too far sometimes, but she would laugh too and hope for the best for his victim. Sometimes after he made fun of someone, he would go over to them and make them feel better about being the target of his joke. Janice thought that made him very noble. At least he thought about how the person must feel. That impressed her. He was popular, dressed in all the newest styles, and he had his own car. He came to school looking as though he just stepped out of a fashion ad for a magazine. Jason was just perfect!

Jason's home life was very much like the life that Janice had lost. Both of his parents were professionals, and they lived in a neighborhood that resembled the one Janice herself lived in when she was younger. He always had lots of money and all the advantages that Janice's family lacked. She was excited when he began to pay her so much attention and called her every day.

Although Jason had all the advantages in life that Janice wished she had, he did not apply himself in class. He barely made the final list for graduation. Janice knew he was smart and capable of being at the top of their class; that was just not one of his priorities. He never had his homework and complained that the teachers cheated him when his grades were low. After signing up to take the SAT the same day as Janice, Jason overslept that morning and did not make it to the testing facility on time. His parents were angry and fussed at him for being lazy, but Janice believed he was just extra tired. His parents were able to make special arrangements for him to take it with a proctor another day. Janice perceived this kind of advantage as extraordinary and fantastic. While she had a job out of necessity, Jason did not need to work, so he spent a lot of time in after-school activities. The Millers believed their son needed extra-curricular activities to help him develop discipline. His family provided him with everything that he needed to develop into a well-rounded individual. Janice saw Jason's life as perfect. Instead of working, he could spend his days on the basketball court and play video games after school. The way she saw it, Jason had a fantastic life.

Janice loved to hear Jason talk about college. When he spoke, he spoke from the vantage point of real-life experience, not like Janice's information from catalogs and websites. His entire family had attended the Biloxi State University in Biloxi, Mississippi. His parents had guided him in the right direction. He was familiar with BSU because his parents had taken him to sports events, homecomings, and graduations. They were financial supporters of the school and knew many of the professors. Jason was well acquainted with all the things about which she had only imagined. He was accustomed to the ends and outs of college life, had visited dormitories, and understood the overall student experience. He had been to Biloxi so many times that he was as familiar with it as he was with their high school. He discussed the sights and places of university life with the ease of people who attended there, lived on campus during those years, and graduated. He even wore the school's shirts with a bold BSU and the school's mascot on it. Janice beamed with admiration when he talked about all the things about which she had only read. He knew the pay scale for the job he would study for in college and what subjects to take that would best serve him in the future. Janice only had second-hand knowledge of those things that she developed from her research and videos.

Janice was a captive audience member when Jason talked about his future and the success he would achieve. He talked a lot about all he was going to do with his life, the exotic places he would live, and the money he would make. Jason told her about his family vacations to different countries and some of the locations of which she had never heard. His family also took him to visit other college campuses, where they went on tours and sat in orientations to make sure he knew where everything was and how to make a good selection. Once he chose his parent's alma mater BSU, they took the time to meet his potential professors and advisors. His parents were substantial financial supporters and used that to Jason's advantage, placing him under those professors' guidance. They pre-planned each semester with electives that would help him be well rounded and knowledgeable about his area of study. They viewed several apartments to see which one would give him the best proximity to everything he would need. He did not need to have a roommate; his parents thought he could concentrate on his studies more if he lived alone. They would foot the bill; of course, they were so happy that he had chosen the school where they were alumni. Janice felt privileged to be able to view this kind of parenting up close. It was all new to her; nothing like this was happening in her world.

Even amidst the excitement in Jason's family about his upcoming college enrollment, Jason was showing signs of disinterest. Because Janice had to fight for every advancement she made, she could not understand his lack of enthusiasm. She listened intently to his stories about his campus excursions and asked questions to help fill in the blanks for what she did not know. It helped her to get current, first-hand information. She continued to make excuses about Jason's apparent laziness and lack of focus. His parents were aggressive in the pursuit of Jason's college career, but he went along with the process with very little input. Janice found herself wishing she could be at the center of that kind of attention, and she certainly could use some help with making all the information assessments that she faced. However, with the lack of leadership from her school administrator, she was pretty much on her own. She learned as much as she could and made the best judgment using what she found.

They were at the end of the school year, and Janice and Jason were spending more and more time together. When they were not together, and she was not working, they were on the phone. They loved being together, and they both liked movies and sports. They attended every basketball, football, and baseball game their team had at home and in nearby cities. They spent every lunch break together at school and talked in the halls as they changed classes. They were wonderful days filled with love and caring. They shared all their thoughts and concerns with one another, and Janice felt as though no one really understood her like Jason.

At times Jason's behavior made Janice uncomfortable. She felt some of the things he did to others were mean. He could even be a little deceitful when he thought it was necessary, but he was so nice to her, so she just overlooked those moments. He was cute and funny, and he never acted that way towards her. His old girlfriend told horror stories about him that Janice did not believe. Jason told her it was just sour grapes! She was just angry because he moved on, and she did not want to see them together. The stories she told of her time dating Jason pictured him as cold and cruel. She had been deeply hurt by him and painted a portrait of him that was not flattering at all. Janice accepted Jason's version, although some of what his old girlfriend said rang true.

With all the time they spent together, she noticed more and more that he was rude routinely to their classmates and people at ticket counters when they went out. What seemed funny to her at the start of their relationship was not so funny now. He could also be irritable and withdrawn, but she understood that he was under so much pressure at home. His parents had strategies for his success and significantly high expectations of him, which in her estimation, was all too much pressure for him. The truth was that Jason's parents were making plans for his future, and he was talking a lot about it as though they were his ideas. Yet, when she looked closely, his parents were planning, and Jason was only talking. In any case, even with the college tours and the conversations concerning his future career, Jason was not applying himself from day to day at school. Janice knew he was smart and able to do the work. She had to study very hard to get good grades, but according to Jason, he did not.

Janice found herself increasingly in the position of having to make excuses for Jason's behavior. Deep down, she believed all he needed was a little encouragement. She just needed to be understanding and show him a little more support. They had gotten so close, and she made it her mission to help him with his schoolwork to raise his GPA. Since she believed that all he needed was a listening ear when he was irritated with his parents, she listened with love.

She fantasized about being his wife and the beautiful home they would have. She planned everything in her imagination: college graduation, fantastic careers, marriage, and of course, three kids in that order. They would live happily ever after; that was what she wished. She craved all the attention he showed her and had fallen quickly and hard for him. Janice felt invisible in her family for so long; his affection towards her was drawing her closer and closer to him. She loved how special he made her feel. Jason found value in her and cared for her. Now the thought of going away to college was harder for her. She did not know how she could bear the separation from Jason for so long. They had moved quickly into a heated romance, and now the time was coming for them to be apart. She did not know how she could bear it.

Jason enjoyed being with Janice a lot and was always

anxious to spend time with her. She was smart and cute. She had meticulously planned her future and was working hard to get there. Her determination to reach her goals, in his estimation, added to her attractiveness. She was precisely the kind of person his parents wanted him to date. Janice had a strong work ethic, and she was enthusiastic and driven to achieve her goals. He admired all those qualities. Secretly, though, he was glad that he did not have it so hard. Jason had visited her home, and it was small and cramped. They did not have much, and he sensed that Janice was a little embarrassed to have him come there. She was usually ready when he came to pick her up, so she rarely asked him to go inside. He was glad about that because he was just a little uncomfortable when he did go inside.

He felt a bit sorry for her and admired her at the same time. She could be a nag about his schoolwork. He silently wished she would concentrate all her efforts on herself and leave him to work out his own life. She could be annoying when she tried to make him work as hard as she did. After all, he was from a different place and could well afford to relax some. His family would take care of the things he fell short of.

Jason's only goal at this point was to enjoy his senior year in high school. It was his last hoorah, and he knew he would have to buckle down and work harder in college. Now all he wanted to do was enjoy his life. He could hardly wait for the end of the school year so that he could have a leisurely summer vacation. The school was honoring all the seniors, and there were several senior events to attend. He was thrilled that it was his turn to be among this elite group. He thought it was too bad that Janice had to work so hard for everything, and some nights she was working and had to miss many of the "senior only" parties. It was regrettable when he had to find another date to take to those functions. It seemed to hurt her feelings a little, and he felt terrible about it, but he did not want to miss the last school dances, and he could not go without a date. High school was supposed to be fun, and she needed to understand that. Then there was the fact that when Janice was not at work, she wanted to study. That was good for her, but he did not have to live like that, and he wasn't going to try. Senior days were fun days, not days to do work, and sometimes Janice just took the work thing too far.

Their romance had gotten serious, and the more time they spent together, the more he wanted to be with her. He imagined her as his first sexual conquest, so he created more situations where they were alone and isolated. Everyone else was already sexually active, but Janice was holding out. While he understood her focus on her goals, they were in love, and people in love had sex. Jason decided to turn up the pressure while knowing that she had religious convictions about sex before marriage, and despite her trying to persuade him that it was right. He could also tell it was getting harder for her to turn him down, so he planned to apply more pressure.

As Jason's feelings for Janice grew, he knew that he did not want to be separated from her for months at a time while they attended different colleges. He started trying to figure out ways they could go to school together. He was aware that his parents had put a lot into preparation for his next step in life, and they were firm in their positions regarding those steps. Janice, on the other hand, had done all her planning by herself; her family was not even involved. He would only have to persuade her that they needed to be together at the same school. It would have to be a good plan because Janice had already put so much into her school search. It would take a lot to turn her around, so this conspiracy would have to be good to change her mind.

He began by suggesting to her that she join him at the university his parents had chosen for him so that they could ride back and forth home together, study together, and continue their wonderful relationship. Biloxi State, where he would attend, did not offer the same major as the one she wanted, they did not have a medical program at all, but she could choose from the other major offerings that were there. The important thing was that they could be together. If he could persuade her to change her direction and go with him to school, he could convince her to move into his apartment with him. Of course, his parents could not know. They would never stand for that.

The first order of business was to convince Janice to come with him. With her work ethic, she could be successful anywhere. The plan would only work if he could get her to change her mind and see things his way. He knew that if they made love, it would solidify and cement their relationship to the degree where she would be easier to convince to do what he wanted her to do and not what she planned to do. He would also promise to marry her, and that would seal the deal; she would not be able to resist his idea then. What started as an idea was slowly becoming Jason's primary goal.

Just about every night, Jason would volunteer to pick Janice up from work. It was convenient for him because he could take his afternoon nap, watch all of his favorite TV shows, and pick her up on time. They could spend the next few hours together, and he did not have to worry about getting sleepy before he drove home. He was free to use those hours with her in his car, talking, cuddling, and changing her mind. Jason was sure he wanted to experience all there was with her. His love for her was overwhelming, and his thoughts pressed him to start their sexual relationship as soon as possible. His insecurities were also taking over; was she saying no because there was someone else? He could not figure it out. He did not understand her resistance to consummating their relationship. Everyone else they knew had already started having sex, and they were closer than ever. He wanted that with Janice. He knew that this would make their relationship stronger; he only had to convince her.

Jason never considered her feelings about religion and God as valid in this instance. After all, God created the whole idea of sex. How could He be against something He created? Wasn't that what happened between people in love? As for her fear of getting pregnant, there was always birth control and, if that failed, abortion. He knew that her arguments were unreasonable and pushed his idea even harder. She was merely acting childish, and her apprehension was unfounded. Once this part of their relationship was in place, Jason knew he could convince her of anything he wanted. He pressed his agenda forward, and there was a lot of work to do to sway her from resisting his plan for them.

Since after work was the only time they had together, Jason fought for as much time with Janice as possible. Surely, Janice could rearrange her schedule and find time to study between classes instead of at night after work. Did she love him the way he loved her? If she did, she would want to be with him during every hour they could manage together as he did. While he admired her work ethic, her time at work was taking away from their time together. He wondered how he could convince her that this much effort was not necessary. She was on her way to college, and soon she would be making lots of money. Right now, all they needed to do was concentrate on building a strong relationship.

The Relationship

God chooses us and wants the best for us. When we follow His direction using His word, life turns out much better. Janice prayed and laid out her entire college career. She consulted God then but is now letting someone who came into her life influence her and change her mind.

Janice is from a broken world where hunger is the norm, and there is not enough of anything to go around. She interprets her education as the ticket out of her situation. She works hard at school to get the best grades that she is capable of and at her job to be the best employee that she can be. Her ambition is to become a professional and change the paradigm of her life. Her time is a valuable commodity, and she is striving to focus on studying and preparing for the next step in her master plan. Janice holds a job to support all the expenses of being a senior and preparing to go away. She cannot expect any help from within her home but is solely dependent on her efforts alone and her ability to plan and execute that plan. She is focused and intentional in all that she does and has meticulously planned every move, investigated every detail, and considered every possible scenario that hinders her progress. She has considered every potential hindrance, that is, except Jason.

Janice met Jason at school and liked him a lot. She considers herself lucky to have met him and is swayed by the fact that someone from such an excellent background, with such a great family, would even consider her to date. He is very attentive to her needs, very kind, and loving in his approach to her. Sure, some days, he is detached and appears to be distracted, but she believes him when he says that he cares for her; his actions agree with his words. He says it over and over, day after day, that he loves her. He picks her up from work and brings her lovely gifts, and as providence would have it, he is the only person in her life who makes her feel loved or even says that to her. She thinks of Jason as the person who is always there for her and always comes to her aid when she needs to talk with someone. He listens to her ideas with interest and offers her sound advice and suggestions. Jason has solidified himself as Janice's confidant and as the one person in her life that she believes loves her without condition.

It is beginning to concern her, though, that he did not seem to understand her need to follow her well-thought-out plan for her life. They would have long talks about what she was going to do, and he offered her advice on the best move to make next. He had been to several campuses and orientations, so he could authoritatively answer some of her questions about what she was facing. However, she noticed that he was not as interested as he should have been about his progress. There was little concern from him about his grades other than merely passing, while she wanted to excel. He slept all afternoon and wanted her to sit up with him after work when she needed to do her homework. He believed that she was overthinking all of this; it was not that hard. It just would not take all the effort she put into it to succeed. He did not seem passionate about anything except starting a sexual relationship with her.

Jason has announced quite casually that he wants her to change her college choice to attend the school his parents chose for him. The problem with that whole idea for Janice is that this was not a small change for her. It would require a change of career focus that she does not want to make. Jason and his family chose a school that lies opposite geographically from that of Janice's choice. Although he had not said it yet, because he keeps referencing his large apartment with no roommate, she knows that he would want her to move into his apartment with him. The arrangement would go against all that her faith and her mother said was right. She wondered, "If he genuinely loved her, why couldn't he understand her need to follow her path and adhere to her faith? If he loved her now, why couldn't their relationship endure the time apart while they both studied to build their future?" These thoughts troubled her and made her feel uneasy.

Jason turned up his pressure on her as they neared the end of the school year to send an application to his school. He was adamant that she would be better off with him at BSU. Janice felt deeply that this was not fair to her, but she did not say aloud what she felt. "Why could he not just go to Johnson State with her?" She wondered. After all, the school she chose had very high ratings and offered his major, as well. He just refused to consider the idea, citing his parents as the reason he could not.

She was feeling stressed and sad when she should have felt relaxed and happy. Something was gnawing at her deep inside. She loved Jason and wanted more than ever for their relationship to work. She did not want to believe that Jason was selfish and manipulating. She did not want to think that he was lazy and just wanted his way. Those thoughts were such a contrast to the amazing feelings she had when they were together. Could she be overthinking this whole thing? Was she simply looking for something about which to be upset? Janice found herself in an anguished state of mind. After feeling unloved for so long, she found someone to love her. Why did it have to be so complicated?

She was being more observant those days and paid more attention to his lack of focus in school and his irresponsible behavior. He seemed to have this view that his parents could fix anything and that if he went to the school they chose, he would have it easy. She often wondered if he was even interested in college at all. She hoped that she could convince him to change his mind and his attitude. Janice believed that if he would go with her to school, she could be there to motivate and encourage him as she did now. Even with all of his shortcomings, he was a very smart person.

His persistence that they start a sexual relationship to strengthen their ties also troubled her. She believed that she should honor God with her body and that it was the temple of the Holy Spirit, which made her uncomfortable with the idea of premarital sex. There was also the risk of unwanted pregnancy and sexually transmitted diseases. She was praying for God's answer and feeling conflicted about her own desires at the same time. A part of her just wanted to go along with him because she cared deeply for him. The other part of her loved God and did not want Him to be disappointed with her behavior. Jason refused to take it into consideration or even try to understand her point of view. If he loved her, she wondered why they could not wait. She was already on track to the education she wanted and needed. Everything was settled and in place. Jason's idea was that it did not matter because they would get married someday, and she would not have to worry about money. His college offered many majors that she could choose from; what was the problem with that? All that mattered, he said, was that they stayed together. The situation was beginning to affect her studies and her concentration.

Temptation

The book of 1st Corinthians, in chapter 15, verse 33, says that evil communications corrupt good manners. Jason has now become the voice in Janice's life to which she listens. She is moving away from well-thought-out hard-earned success and goals for herself. What voices are you listening to that can bring life-changing results to you?

With graduation at long last behind them, the first leg of

Janice's plan is complete. She gave in to Jason's desire for a sexual relationship and applied to his college for admittance. What he said seemed right; it bonded them even closer together than ever. At first, she felt guilty, but as time passed, she began to put her guilty feelings in the past and moved forward. They were in love and refocused themselves together, merging their futures and planning their lives. Janice felt, it was so much nicer not doing all of the planning on her own.

Her research on the expenses she would encounter was useless now because everything changed with her decision to follow Jason. Jason assured her that she would not have to work as many hours as she would have if she were alone and without support in a strange city. With the two of them in an apartment furnished by his parents, she only needed spending change because his parents shouldered all of his expenses, and they could share his car. Janice could not be happier that she had a partner in her quest for a new life.

BSU accepted Janice almost immediately; her grades and her scores were excellent. She was clueless as to what her major should be; trying to find something close to her original choice was not easy. Jason told her that it was all a part of starting their lives together, and when his career took off, she only had to work after graduation if she wanted to, so why was she worried? His mother worked because it was her choice, not out of necessity for the family to live well. Janice was concerned because she wanted a major that she would enjoy, one for which she had some passion. Janice consoled herself with the idea that she would still have the education her mother warned her was the best way to restore her life to normal. She would still get to leave home on time. She comforted herself with those thoughts.

Her feelings wavered from anxiety over changing her major

to excitement about being with Jason. She already crossed that sexual threshold with him, and he seemed more in love with her than ever. She struggled most when she was in prayer or at church. During those times, she felt guilty, as though she had violated her relationship with God. It was easier not to think about it at all because those moments only brought doubt and fear about her next move, so she pushed everything out of her mind. When she did not control her thoughts, many, many warning bells were going off, enough bells for a concert. She believed that it was just because she did not have her new path well thought out as she had before. When she was with Jason, everything felt good and promising, but when she was alone, her doubts would not stop pestering her.

Fall arrived, it was time to leave for college, and Janice's family was very excited. Her mother had been somewhat resistant as she contemplated going to another school at Jason's urging. She questioned why she would make such a drastic change after she had spent so much time planning what she wanted for her life. Her mother said, "If Jason loves you, he will still love you while you finish college." Mother reminded her, "Love should not be contingent upon being together all of the time." The kind of love that would last a lifetime could withstand the separation as they built a solid foundation for their futures, was what her mother believed.

Nevertheless, Janice pressed ahead, visualizing a life with Jason and the secret marriage he promised. Soon she and Jason could be together all the time, and she would never have to worry about feeling unloved again. She could help him with his studies and motivate him when he stalled. They were good together.

They planned their deception carefully and decided that Jason would leave on schedule for school with his parents in tow. His parents were traveling with him to help him settle into his new apartment. They rented a small van to bring his belongings from home and scheduled themselves to stay two days to make sure everything was in place in his new environment. His rented furniture would be delivered the day they arrived. They would take him grocery shopping and help him unpack his things. Classes would begin the next week, and his parents wanted to ensure that domestic chores did not hamper his progress. The excitement that they believed was his enthusiasm for school was actually his excitement over moving in with Janice and having her all to himself. Jason played the role his parents expected of him, like a thespian on stage. He always did.

While his parents were unpacking and giving him their last instructions, Jason was daydreaming about the next two days when Janice would arrive. He was happy that he was able to convince Janice to come to BSU. He did not have to worry so much about starting college life alone. The truth was that the idea had never appealed to him. He would have chosen to stay at home and go to the local college, but his parents felt as if living on his own at school with their oversight and mentoring would help mature him and help him be more accountable for his well-being. They wanted this experience to move him from his lazy ways to a hard-working, sensible adult. They told him, "That is what the college experience is all about, moving from childhood to adulthood. There, he would gradually be weaned from everyday parental oversight and learn to take on adulthood with them as his safety net. "If they only knew," he thought.

After graduation from high school, Jason's parents believed that he would emerge from college with everything he needed to be a successful adult, or so they thought. He would have the opportunity to live on his own and manage a household, study without their urging, and become the strong young man they knew he could be. Jason had already arranged not to be alone. He did not feel guilty like Janice did. He was calm and collected as he went through the motions of deceit with his parents. He said all the right things and asked all the right questions. He did not want anything to happen that would make them suspicious or cause them to stay another day.

Meanwhile, Janice was packed and ready to leave home to arrive there the same evening his parents left. She would leave home a few hours before his parents left on their trip back home. It was just a nine-hour ride by bus. She and Jason had calculated it well. He had even bought her a bus ticket. She would take the bus and arrive late that night. Jason would pick her up from the bus station, and they would go to their new apartment.

His parents had made sure that everything was in place at his apartment. She would only have to unpack and settle in. They would never suspect that she was moving in. Jason assured her that everything would be okay. They would start their lives together early. Janice knew parents on both sides would vehemently disapprove. She told her mother that she would be living in the dorm. She felt bad about the deception, but since she and Jason had promised a secret marriage soon, she consoled herself that all would be well.

Janice overrode all her feelings of doubt and left for school as planned. She moved in with Jason. Together they picked a suitable major for her and the corresponding classes she needed. She settled into Jason's apartment and fantasized about how she would redecorate. She wanted it to reflect some of her taste since she was moving in. His parents were exceptionally generous; they had let Jason pick everything for his apartment. It seemed much too masculine for her taste. Right away, she had mentally started decorating their first place together. She wanted it to reflect their collective taste.

Classes would start the next week with them as a couple, and she was happier than ever. She pushed their deceptive lifestyle to the back of her mind. What their parents did not know would not hurt them. After their marriage and graduation, they would tell them the story of how they lived together during college. It would just be a story they could laugh at, or so she hoped. The fact that they were together was all that mattered; she had received the reward of true love early. Janice never pictured herself in this position; living with a man without marriage was never in her mind as something she would do. The move in with Jason was earlier than she had planned and out of the order of her original thoughts. Nevertheless, so what if the plan was out of order? It was working out, and they were happy.

They settled into life together quite well. Janice cooked, cleaned, and more often than she wanted to, helped Jason with his homework. Even in college, he was lax with his academic career. He would wait until the last minute to do his projects or write a paper, and Janice would have to jump in and save the day. Only now, she could no longer make excuses for him. It was apparent to her now that Jason had enough time to do his work. He did not have to work or do anything around the house and could have gotten things done on time. Janice tried giving him gentle reminders, which he found irritating, but he knew if he were rude enough, she would stop her nagging. Jason continued to be as he had done in high school, barely passing.

Janice was exasperated when she had to write his papers completely. Doing Jason's work was sometimes hard on her because she had her class load to carry, not to mention housework, and she viewed representing her work as his work as dishonest. He did not seem to have a problem with that. Although it remained unsaid, it was always in the back of her mind that she was living in

HIS apartment free. She did not feel that she was in a position to demand anything. While she was grateful that the significant expense of housing was not on her plate, after some time, Janice came to wish she had moved into the dorm on campus and not into Jason's apartment. Some days she felt as though Jason treated her like the live-in housekeeper. He often pointed out that her cleaning was not according to his schedule, or maybe it was not cleaned up to his standard. Mentally she thought, "If you don't like it, do it yourself," however, she did not dare say it aloud.

Living with Jason had taught her that the bite of his words that she witnessed toward their high school classmates seemed harsher when he directed them towards her. She found out by personal experience that his former girlfriend had been telling the truth about many things she said about Jason. She regretted that she had not listened. Amazingly, with all she had to do, Janice still made excellent grades.

Then there was yet another gnawing thought; she initially moved in thinking there would soon be a marriage proposal, at least that is what he promised her. That was all Jason talked about before they left home. Now when she brought it up, he seemed irritated and did not want to talk about it at all. When he did answer her questions about marriage, he would say things like, "Oh, we have plenty of time." Janice wondered how she allowed herself to end up in this position. She had trapped herself and taken away her power to choose. The promise which had influenced her decision most to move into this situation was that there would be an early marriage. These days she felt like the marriage was getting further and further away.

Reflective Questions

1. What are three problems living by emotions could cause?

2. Is it ever a good idea to make major life changes based on emotions? Why/Why not?

3. Consider the relationships in your life. Is there any person who could sabotage the goals that you have for yourself?

4. Do you need to invite God into the plans you are making for yourself?

Prayer

Father, show me your ways and lead me in the paths that I should go. Help me to remember your great love for me. You know all about my past and my future. Give me wisdom as I prepare to take hold of the future that you have prepared for me. Heavenly Father, I submit myself to you. Help me to see the value you place on me.

Chapter 3
Redemption

Love does not dishonor   1 Corinthians 13:5

But you are the ones chosen by God, chosen for the high calling of priestly work, chosen to be a holy people, God's instruments to do his work and speak out for him, to tell others of the night-and-day difference he made for you—from nothing to something, from rejected to accepted.   **1 Peter 2:9-10**

Janice settled in, started her classes, and as the days turned to months, she noticed she was doing more and more of Jason's homework, not just a paper here and there. Now, for any class they went to together, she needed two perspectives on every homework assignment, one for herself and one for Jason. Janice was smart enough to pick the best topics and projects for herself. She would try to motivate him, but his attitude would change, and he would barely speak to her after one of her "encouragement talks." "You do your life, and I'll do mine," he would say. "We are supposed to be in this together, right?" Janice pondered.

After months of that kind of frustration, she found a nice church to join. Her faith had sustained her when she was at home. She started attending a great one during her senior year in high school and wanted to regain her momentum. For her, it was the right thing to do. She remembered all the lessons she learned when her Granddad took her to church. From her childhood, she always practiced prayer and talked to God regularly. She felt a little guilty now because to get rid of the shame brought on by their agreed-upon deception, she stopped attending church, and her prayer life greatly diminished when she moved in with Jason. After she met Jason, she slowed down and nearly stopped anything spiritual. She could see now that so many things in her life had changed since she started dating Jason. She changed everything she wanted to please him. She had always been fiercely independent, and now she felt more like a puppet. "How did I get here?" she questioned. Her happy ending was not feeling so happy after all.

Jason wanted no part of organized religion. He said he could pray while he slept-in on Sunday. He could not see why she needed to go at all, either. If God was everywhere and could hear your prayers, why was it necessary to go to a church to pray? His parents had forced him to go when he was at home. Now that he was on his own, Jason did not see the necessity to leave home on his free weekends. Maybe he would leave home if there was a game or if someone asked them over, but other than that, he needed to regroup. He needed that time to rest, recuperate, and enjoy some leisure activities. However, he continued to lie to his parents and say he was attending church when they called. Sometimes when he was talking with his parents, Janice felt like she could not believe her ears. Jason thought it was funny, and he would rave about his performance after he hung up from speaking with them.

Time seemed to drag now, and the better she got to know him, the more she wondered how she missed so much about Jason. In her low moments, she just felt used! Had she been insane? When her attitude became evident, he would make new promises. To appease her, Jason said he would tell his parents about her living there. He only said it during one of their "What Happened to the Early Marriage" talks, but so far, it had not happened. She was concerned about that, too. Even if she had to endure the shame of his parents knowing that she lived there with Jason, she wanted to stop living every day of her life in a lie. It would also be a relief if she did not feel she was an embarrassment to him. What would they think of her if they knew the truth? Her feelings were conflicted because she did not want to lie anymore, but she also did not want his parents to think of her as anything except a nice girl. When she thought about it, she queried herself thinking, were her actions those of a nice girl, and had she removed herself from the "Nice Girl" category with this deception? If his parents knew, would she have to move? The dorms were full now, and she could not afford an apartment alone. Where would she go?

Janice hated the times when his parents visited because she had to find somewhere to go! To top that off, she had to take most of her things and pack them in the (she hesitated to use the word *our*) apartment's storage unit, and what couldn't fit in the storage unit she hid under the bed. Then she would either check into a hotel or stay with a friend. These moments always caused her to feel cheap and used. She thought it was good that her mother could not come to visit because that would be a problem of great magnitude. Because how could she keep her from finding out the truth? She made enough money to send to her, but her living arrangement was not what she wanted her mother to see. She used a post office box for any mail from her family; the deceit was gnawing at her most of the time. Whenever Janice summoned her courage, she talked with Jason about her conflicting emotions. These days when she brought it up, he would leave the apartment after asking her to stop nagging him. He told her he had enough on his mind. His parents were nagging him about his grades, the professors were not grading fairly, and she wanted to get married. He did not need more pressure from her; he would yell. More and more, he started spending time away from the apartment, leaving home early and coming home late. Janice wondered where all the love he professed for her had gone. She did not see much of it these days. What could she do? She felt trapped. Why had she not listened to her reservations about moving here?

Revelation

Jason had a project due in two days, and once again, he had yet to come home. Janice thought of a fantastic idea for a project that he could do in a short time, but where was he? She was accustomed to helping him with his assignments and shopped after her classes to pick up everything he needed to get it done. Sometimes, when he had an assignment due, it caused her to be under pressure because she had little time to do her assignments by the time she helped him with his project, especially if they were in a class they took together. This time she decided to be proactive.

She read his syllabus to find out what he needed to turn in, and she went shopping to secure the items it would take to complete the project according to specification. She laid everything out on the kitchen table so he could get started when he got home. In her mind, it was so fraudulent to give him as much help as she was giving him. She did not mind helping Jason but resented it when most of the prep work for the assignment fell on her shoulders. It irritated her that he had come to expect her to do all of his prep work and that this behavior had become the norm for him. Janice wanted them to have a great future and realized that a lot of their success in their chosen professions would be dependent on how well they did in college. She rationalized that helping him was working on her future as well.

It was getting late, and Jason was not answering his cell phone. Exasperated, she decided to go out and find him so they could get his assignment finished that night. She hated it when he tried to complete a project the morning it was due; he would be irritable and difficult. He even expected her to miss her morning class, if necessary, to finish his assignment. It would be to her advantage to find him and urge him to come home now. There were only a few places on campus where he hung out, and she was familiar with all of them. She had a big exam tomorrow and needed time to study for herself; if she pushed him across the finish line, she would have enough time for her assignments without too much stress and pressure. She reasoned that his phone must have been dead because her calls were going directly to voicemail. After leaving five messages, she knew she had to find him, it was getting late, and she did not want to stay up all night helping him while he complained about his fatigue. He always forgot the due dates on his projects and never checked the calendar she hung over the kitchen table that she continually updated with their assignment deadlines.

Janice grabbed her coat, jumped into her car, and drove toward campus. She was happy that she managed to find a car so cheap. Sharing a car with Jason became difficult shortly after she arrived and moved in. She could use it when there was an advantage in it for him or if they were going somewhere together, but not if it was solely for her benefit. He was against her buying her a car for herself, probably because it gave her some independence from him. Hers was an old car, a blue compact, and not very pretty, but it got her where she needed to go. She had the motor checked out when she bought it, so she knew it was solid and would last a long time. She believed that if she took care of it, this car would be enough transportation until she could graduate and get a job. Janice always had excellent money management skills, mostly because there had not been much money in her home. She learned early not to be wasteful or overspend. Whatever money she had, she needed to make good use of it. Her job was close to their apartment, but she needed a reliable ride to get home at night. Until now, she depended on Jason to get around town, and he was becoming increasingly unreliable.

A couple of nights, he was more than an hour late picking her up, and one night she even walked home. It was an excellent decision to spend the money. Reliable transportation was essential to her success. She drove towards campus in silence, not turning on the radio. She did this sometimes when she needed to think through situations or center her emotions after a round with Jason. Tonight, she focused on how she would approach him to come home without him making a scene. He could be crude with his comments when he had an audience. She had to prepare a response that would leave her with some dignity, just in case.

For her first stop, she went to his friend Sam's apartment. Sam befriended Jason when they were both new on campus. He was from Michigan and a long way from family and friends. He and Jason met during freshman orientation and had the same academic advisor. They were sitting outside her office waiting, and through conversation, they found they had a lot in common. He was one of Jason's closest friends since they arrived at BSU. They had the same majors, and a couple of their classes were together. When she reached his apartment, Sam said he had not seen Jason since their class together and suggested she try one of his favorite places to eat. When she approached the diner and recognized his car, she was relieved, "Good," she thought. I do not have to keep looking; it is late, I am tired, and he has not even started his project. She found a parking space close to his anticipating that they would walk back to their cars together. After she parked the car, she got out and walked swiftly toward the front door.

The diner had a large window that covered most of the front of the building, reaching about one foot above the ground with a large plate of their signature burger combo on it. There were several students at the tables outside, eating, talking, and some just hanging out. One table of students seemed to be in a study group, but Janice knew it would take a miracle to find Jason with that particular crowd. There were a few people she recognized from her classes sitting outside talking. They looked at each other as she approached and hesitantly spoke to Janice. It was not their usual friendly greeting to which she had grown accustomed. Their looks made her just a little uneasy, and they talked to each other in hushed tones as she passed. She did not think much of it at the time because she was so focused on finding Jason. She spoke and did not slow down or break her stride to chat; she was on a mission. After she walked past them, she felt a little strange, "I wonder what that was about?" she thought. Something about their demeanor was unsettling. Janice checked her clothes, trying not to look obvious; she had not put on any makeup when she left the apartment. She was usually so meticulous about how she presented herself. They had not seen her before with her around-the-house look. She was a little embarrassed that they must have noticed. "I should have taken more time to check my appearance out before I left the house, "I won't do that again," she mused.

She quickly brushed off the encounter and refocused. She was on a mission. She searched for Jason's face through the diner's window as she entered the front door. She pushed the restaurant door wide and felt a chill as her stomach went queasy. She saw a familiar figure in a booth with his back toward her, but this person was sitting with a girl, and he had his arm around her. They were laughing and seemed to be having a great time. The girl must have said something amusing because he kissed her gently on the cheek and laughed loudly. It was Jason's voice and Jason's laugh, she reasoned as she stood there for a moment, spellbound, almost frozen in time. Frozen in a moment that made her heart pound, her face was hot with embarrassment even while she began to process the scene before her. She suddenly understood why their classmates looked at her the way they did and greeted her haltingly outside. They knew what she was about to encounter. They knew she lived with Jason and that they had come to school together. It was too late to run and too late to act as if she did not see him. Her world was crashing down, her hopes disintegrating, and she wanted to scream. She slowed her pace as if in slow motion, and as she drew closer, as her heart sank even further. She did not want to believe her eyes. Their eyes met. Her heart sank deeper as she remembered all the nights he said he was working on projects or out with Sam. "How long had this been going on?" she wondered.

Janice's impulse was to run away, and she felt as if everyone had stopped what they were doing to watch the confrontation. When she finally reached the table, she felt lost for what to say or do next. He looked at her and spoke to her as if nothing was unusual about the situation that was currently unfolding. His demeanor was friendly, and the smile never left his face. She knew Jason was a smooth operator and a liar. I wonder how he will explain this episode. She was aware of her heartbeats with each moment she stood there. She stared silently at first and then found her voice, "Jason, who is this?" she tried to make her voice steady and lighthearted. He went into an introduction as if Janice was just a casual friend. He addressed the girl he was with, "Amy, this is Janice; she is from my hometown. We went to high school together." Still not believing the situation she found herself in, with her stomach about to fail her, Janice muttered a single word, "Hi," and gracefully turned and walked away. Jason knew her well enough to know that she would not make a scene; he could depend on her passive personality for a quiet departure from the restaurant. He would deal with her later. Janice looked back as she exited the diner and saw Jason with his arm still around Amy, and they were laughing as if nothing had happened.

Once she was out of view of the audience at the diner, Janice was so upset that she ran back to their apartment, leaving her car behind. Her heart ached, and tears burned her face. What had just happened? She did not want to trust her emotions after what she had just encountered. She did not want to believe what she saw! What she had just seen changed everything that she had convinced herself was true. Was this the actions of someone who loved her? What kind of future was this behavior promising? An hour ago, she was setting up Jason's project and anticipating her study time for her upcoming exam. She was in their apartment, working toward their future together and their eventual marriage. Now what? She reached the apartment, let herself in, and waited for Jason. She needed to understand, and she needed an explanation that would not insult her intelligence. Somewhere inside, she knew there was none. What she had just witnessed was exactly what it appeared to be. She could not fool herself. Jason was cheating; she could not rationalize it away. Now what? She cried until she did not have any tears left, and after that, only a periodic groan came from somewhere inside her as she watched the door for him to come home for what seemed like an eternity.

Jason completed his date with Amy Elliott without rushing. They met about two months earlier when a class assignment put them on the same team. He liked her a lot, and they had so much in common. Amy lived on campus, and he started walking her to her dorm from the library so he could spend a little more time with her after their group study session. She was both interesting and funny. When he was with her, he felt he could escape, if only for a little while, the confines of living with Janice. Her insistence that he spend all his free time studying and the annoying way she brought up marriage at least once a month was just too much. It was taking the fun out of their relationship and his college experience. He could have stayed at home with his parents if he wanted that kind of nagging. Although he liked Janice a lot, too, he had not counted on how driven she was about her future and her studies. Her obsession with saving money was irritating, too. She never seemed to relax and go with the flow. Amy, on the other hand, was from a family more like his; they sent her a generous allowance, and she did not have to work. Her family traveled a lot, and they talked about all of the places they each had visited. Interestingly enough, they had been to several of the same NFL games with their families. She was calm, cool, and easy to be around.

Jason was unsure how he would handle the confrontation he knew was inevitable when he got home. It was one of her problems; Janice always tried to make him be more like her. He had gotten very skilled at shutting Janice down with his lack of responses to her questions. Tonight, he would not address what happened, and in the morning, he would tell Janice his parents were coming in the day after tomorrow, and she had to make herself scarce for the weekend. What he would not do is explain who Amy was and that being with her caused him to be late coming home these days. He expected Janice to grill him, but he would not answer. Janice could draw any conclusions she wanted; he was a single man and did not have to answer her like they were married. It was a good thing that he did not give her an engagement ring. As it stood, she was just a girlfriend like any other girlfriend that he had ever dated. Janice was a nice girl and everything, but they were very different in their perspectives on life. He saw some of it when they were at home, but living with her was even more intense than he ever contemplated it would be. He envisioned them living together, going to classes, and enjoying everything about the collegiate experience. He did not count on her being so obsessed with her future until it drained all of the fun out of her. He had no intention of wasting all of his university years in the books when passing grades worked just as well.

He could quickly kill two birds with one stone. Janice would have time to calm down by the time she spent a weekend away from his apartment. On the other hand, Amy, whom he had foolishly invited to come over Saturday night, would finally be able to see the apartment he had been hiding from her. "He could do whatever he wanted to; after all, it was his apartment," he thought. Janice never left any of her things visible, so his plan should work out perfectly.

Jason arrived at his apartment an hour later. Janice did not speak right away; she was waiting for an apology and an explanation. Without looking her in the eye or even bringing up what had happened, he looked at her and decided to take charge of the conversation. I see you left your car at the diner; how did you get home? "I walked," was her only reply. He looked at the table where the supplies for his project were lying. "Thanks for getting all of that for me. I will start on it in the morning." "It's due in the morning, Jason," Janice said with an edge in her voice. "That is why I came looking for you." She was still waiting for him to initiate a conversation about Amy, but he did not. While she was searching for somewhere to begin asking the question that was hanging heavily in the air between them, he turned to face her. He matter-of-factly said, "My parents will be here this weekend, so you need to move your things and call one of your friends to see if you can stay over for a couple of days."

Janice could hardly process what she was hearing! No apology, no explanation, "Who was that girl, Jason? Janice asked hesitantly. Jason's reply was cold and unfeeling, "You know who she is; I introduced you to her. I do not feel like answering a whole lot of questions tonight, and my parents will be here the day after tomorrow. Try to clear out by tomorrow afternoon; see if Sharon is okay with you staying over." Sharon was the best friend Janice had at school. She did not care much for Jason and tried to tell Janice he was holding her back. As Janice watched, Jason turned without another word and started getting ready for bed.

Sharon Harris

Sharon Harris was from a small town in Wisconsin and enrolled in school on an academic scholarship. She came here to study interior design, and this school offered a great program in that field. For her minor, she chose Visual Arts to enhance her marketability. If she did well in these courses, there was also a possibility that she could earn an internship with one of the best interior design firms in the country. Her strategy would ensure that she would end up in New York, where she desperately wanted to live and practice her craft. The competition was fierce in New York, but success was certainly possible with talent and hard work. Everywhere she went, she would study the rooms and the décor in each one of them. She would mentally redecorate each room. She did this as far back as she could remember; she paid attention to the shape and size of the room, the color of the walls, the flooring, and the window treatments. She imagined how she would decorate the room and all the changes she would make. Everyone said it was her gift to decorate while she knew it was more than that; it was a passion.

Sharon applied for and received an efficiency apartment in the new dorms designed for those who did not desire a roommate. The suite was a part of the dormitory system but was larger than a typical dorm room with a kitchenette, living area, and bath. Living there meant she had the freedom and quiet to study whenever she wanted. She preferred to study late at night or about four in the morning, which can be inconvenient when you have a roommate. Her parents had purchased a comfortable, oversized leather chair with a pullout, twin-sized bed. That was helpful when her younger sister wanted to come to visit her during a big game or other campus festivities. She was happy to let Janice stay there when she needed to; it was the least she could do to help her.

Sharon met Janice on their first day at BSU as they headed to orientation and registration. When Janice and Jason walked to the campus auditorium, they ended up walking side by side with Sharon in tandem up the front steps of the building. They started a conversation, and Janice introduced the person to her as Jason, her boyfriend. Janice told her that she and Jason dated in high school and came to BSU together. They both looked eager and thrilled to be on a new adventure as a couple. Sharon immediately liked Janice, so they exchanged contact information and agreed to meet for lunch sometimes. Jason, on the other hand, although he seemed kind enough, gave her a feeling she did not like. The looks he gave her when Janice was not looking were not at all innocent. She avoided eye contact and any direct conversation with him from that day forward. She felt sorry for Janice that first day, sensing her sincerity and Jason's obvious insincerity.

Sharon and Janice continued to communicate as the semester went on, often had lunch together, and became very good friends and confidants. Janice confided in her about her dissatisfaction with her living arrangements and how complicated her life was because of their common deception toward their parents. She further revealed her regret and disillusionment with her relationship with Jason. She was happy to find a friend with whom she could be honest. Her living situation was often depressing and overwhelming. She would never let herself see her predicament as a mistake because that would be more than she could bear. That would take her into an abyss of having to acknowledge all that she gave up following an illusion. She would have to admit that she believed a lie; Jason had also deceived her. It was just easier to ride it out and hope for the best. Still, when she did get venting time with her new friend, she found relief when she could, if only for a little while, not pretend her life was great, or lie about her situation. Janice was smart, studied hard, and her imminent career was very promising.

Jason, Sharon learned over time, was lazy, did not want to study, and getting by was good enough for him. These traits were in direct conflict with Janice, who strove for perfection in her academic and personal endeavors. Jason promised her so much and had given her so little. Although Janice never voiced it, Sharon knew that deep inside was a thought that Janice would not allow to surface. Based on their conversations, she knew that Janice feared what would happen if it all fell apart.

It was not surprising to Sharon the first time Janice called looking for a place to stay. Janice shared her living situation, and she knew that Janice did not have very much money to spend on hotels. She also knew that Jason did not help her financially whenever she was forced to stay overnight in a hotel. Sharon was happy to help Janice and was glad her parents had the forethought to purchase the comfortable leather chair with the pullout bed. It was perfect for Janice, and she was glad she could be there for her. She could not understand why Janice could not see that Jason was an insincere jerk. After a couple of weeks in school, almost every freshman girl on campus knew his name. He oozed what he believed to be charm, but Sharon found his demeanor disgusting. She was careful, though, to listen to Janice without passing judgment on Janice or giving her negative opinions about Jason. Janice was embarrassed to ask and felt bad enough about this imposition as it was. She made up her mind to be a friend; Janice was going to need someone soon, she surmised. Hopefully, she would see who Jason was before it wrecked her life.

Sharon did not think much of Jason, not just because of the over-friendly way he sometimes looked at her or that he flirted with any girl who would listen, but she also did not care for the way he treated Janice. Janice did not seem to notice his waywardness, and it was none of her business, but Jason talked to her as though she was less than intelligent. His personality screamed that he was an entitled, spoiled brat. After they met that first day going to the freshmen orientation, Sharon had seen Jason chatting up several girls. She learned quickly, however, that Janice was not open to hearing anything negative about Jason. She made an excuse for every one of Jason's bad behaviors. Sharon decided, as a good friend, to listen and help her as much as possible. She worried about her new friend, though.

The Fallout

Janice went to bed that night feeling numb. Jason felt like a stranger to her at that moment. She had compromised so much and re-arranged her entire future. She had changed her college and her major and given up her long-awaited independence, all for love. What troubled her most was that she had compromised her relationship with God. And for what? She now questioned whether it was ever really love at all or just the desperation to leave home, coupled with her heart's desire for total acceptance. She began her trek into the dating world believing that premarital sex was not the best choice, but Jason had convinced her that it would lead to their marriage and happily ever after. She believed that if she did what he wanted, she would eventually get what she needed. Her desire was to be loved and have a normal, ideal family again like the one she had lost. Janice felt as though her entire life had unraveled in the last few hours. Stirring deep in her heart, though, was the truth; she had foolishly traded all that she believed in for a counterfeit love experience that failed her. As Janice lay awake that night, her thoughts turned to where she would go. She only had a few hours to gather her things and find somewhere to spend the next few days alone. Her friend Sharon usually allowed her to stay at her place when she did not have other guests. She did not want to call Sharon, though, because she was the person who kept telling her that Jason was using her.

Sharon had gently tried to open her eyes to Jason, but Janice would not listen. Deep inside, she knew that what Sharon was telling her was the truth. She did not want to face her now. Even if "I told you so" was never spoken, it would be the elephant in the room. What other options did she have? She had spent most of her money on her car, so her savings accounts had low balances. She was in an awful predicament. Janice marveled at how she had gotten to this place. She was living in a lie, and it appeared that the lie was a lot deeper than she ever wanted to believe. She doubted if anything Jason said to her was ever true. She questioned if things could ever feel good again.

Janice remembered her childhood prayers. She started to talk to God again that night. She stopped praying when she moved in with Jason because he would comment about how silly prayer was and how unnecessary he believed it to be. He would point out his life and all that he had, although he never prayed, then he would contrast her life with so little and how hard she had to work to get by. "So, how is prayer helping you?" He would ask. Also, to contend with was the fact that prayer would inevitably bring on guilty feelings, and her thoughts would start to condemn her. But eventually, she began to attend church again, ignoring Jason's comments and her guilty feelings. Jason made her feel silly about her faith when they were at home, and he was pressuring her for sex. She did not think it was right to deceive their parents, but she allowed him to change her mind. She started to rationalize, "A lot of the students lived together to save money." Janice now realized that rationalizing as she abandoned her values was her first step into this disaster.

Her mother had often spoken against living together before marriage, saying that the young man and his family would lose their respect for her. Tonight, however, she remembered God's word more than the condemnation she felt. She whispered, "He is faithful and just to forgive and cleanse you from all unrighteousness." Her hope had to be in Him. She fell asleep that night, praying and praising Him for the answer to her dilemma. After all, she had entrusted all her hopes and desires from childhood to Him until the decision that brought her to this awful moment.

The morning after seeing Jason with Amy, he left the apartment, leaving Janice feeling abandoned and alone. Her physical heart felt heavy, and her thoughts were swirling. The questions she had so often pushed away were coming into her mind like they were bullets fired from an automatic rifle. How could he be so cold? How long had this been going on? He wanted her to move her things by tomorrow afternoon. Up to now, she always knew well in advance when his parents were coming; they planned her time away from the apartment together. What did this all mean? Were the Millers actually coming, or was Jason lying? She did not know how to process what happened last night because he refused to talk about it, and she did not know how to perceive his actions this morning. Never had she felt so devastated; never had she felt so alone. She dragged herself out of bed and slowly started the ritual for which she had gotten a lot of practice during the first semester, collecting her things so that Jason's parents would not know she was living there. He usually helped her, but he left much earlier than usual that morning. He got up, barely said good morning, dressed quickly, and left the apartment.

Her heart ached because of Jason's indifference to her distress. Jason was cold and distant, which made Janice feel as though maybe when she left this time, he might not allow her to return. His behavior with Amy caught her by surprise. She did not know he was capable of this kind of cruelty. Did she know him at all?" she wondered. Naively she allowed herself to believe that telling their parents a lie was a first for them; at least, it was for her. She had seen him treat others poorly and watched his selfish indifference to his brothers and sisters, but she was feeling the full brunt of what it was like to be on the receiving end of Jason's narcissistic behavior.

She moved about the apartment slowly, and then clarity overtook her. Since Jason could not be trusted, why not call his mother for herself, and verify his story? Did he forget, or was he trying to have a free weekend? Unsure she could handle the truth, she hesitantly picked up the phone and called Jason's mother. Mrs. Miller answered the phone cheerily and was happy to hear from Janice. She asked Janice about how her classes were going and told her she had spoken with her mother just the other day. After a lot of small talk, the conversation then turned to Jason's siblings and how they were doing in school. When after several minutes into their discussion, there was no mention of their impending visit, Janice gathered her nerve and decided to ask the question to which she had been dreading the answer. Janice plunged forward but with apprehension. "I would love to see you; when will you be here?' she asked. "We aren't coming again until close to the end of the semester because our schedule is so heavy," was her reply. Janice sank even deeper into the chair. Her greatest fear was happening. Mrs. Miller confirmed Jason wasn't asking her to move her things because his parents were coming that weekend! Why was he asking her to move her belongings? It was yet another lie in the string of lies he had already told her.

Janice finished packing and sat quietly in a large, oversized chair next to the window. She often sat in this chair when she studied. It was comfortable and had a large table next to it with a lamp that was perfect for studying and meditating. There were several decisions for her to make today; this was no time to collapse into helplessness and despair. She felt deflated and defeated but somehow empowered. She recognized this as her avenue of escape. It was Jason who had convinced her to come here, and Jason gave her the motivation she needed to leave for good.

Janice slipped back into her old familiar planning mode. She had very little money to plan her exit from this situation. What would she do now, where would she go, and how could she achieve a positive outcome even while she was in pain? There was an immediate need to leave and no place for her to go. It was funny; the home that she had been so anxious to leave looked good to her now. Should she call her mother and ask for help? That would mean telling her all about the deceit and her significant failure. The harsh truth was that she did not want to return home even if her mother allowed her to come home. She had to figure out another way, and time was running out. Jason would be home soon, or would he? Janice wanted to be gone whenever he returned. For the first time in their relationship, she prayed that he would stay away from the apartment. She needed time to plan and think through the possibilities of her next move.

Her thoughts returned to her original plan for her future and the steps she took to overcome the roadblocks that she encountered. She knew what to do and how to construct a solid plan for herself. She would have to draw on her rational, methodical personality traits to figure her way out of this situation. One thing was clear to her; this moment was the catalyst that she needed to change her life.

Her need for love led her down this path. The question for her now was how to get back on the right track. As she agonized over her mistakes, she realized that she had ignored all the warning signs that were readily available for her to see. They were all there in plain sight. She made excuses for Jason's laziness and poor treatment of others, rationalized his explanations, and overlooked his bad behavior toward his own family. She must now face the hard truth of all those actions. She knew that God loved her, and God's love brought an expectation for her behavior. He gave specific instructions in His word. Janice acknowledged that she compromised her covenant with God so that Jason would not leave her. Didn't the bible say that love never fails? She had become sexually active with him at his urging. Now he was moving on with someone else, and the love that she thought he had for her had dissipated.

Reflective Questions

1. How could Janice be blinded to what was clearly visible to others concerning Jason's behavior?

2. Why do you think Janice could not see that Jason's pursuit of her was selfishly motivated?

3. What are the areas in your own life where you might have developed an inability to see situations that could cause you to make decisions that are not in your best interest?

Prayer

Lord, help me to be conscious of the areas in my life that might cause me to make decisions that are not balanced with wisdom. Thank you for ordering every step in all areas of my life.

Chapter 4
Redemption

Love does not remember wrongs done against it. 1 Corinthians 13:5

Courage to Move Forward

Janice did a lot of thinking and planning that morning. She had mistaken Jason's lust for love. It was now time to stop pretending she was happy and make some hard choices, ones that, until now, she did not allow herself to contemplate. As she sat in the chair that morning, she knew she would make several life-changing decisions, and she had a short time to make them. Jason said that he only wanted her to move her things temporarily, but did she even want to come back? She sat for what seemed like hours going over which decisions, one by one, had brought her to this place. She had to analyze them carefully so that she would never make those mistakes again. It seemed as if clarity was seeping slowly into her thinking process. She could comprehend things that she had only "seen" before.

As her thinking cleared, Janice picked up a Bible that was sitting next to her on a table and read:
"Stay joined together with me and follow my teachings. If you do this, you can ask for anything you want, and it will be given to you. Show that you are my followers by producing much fruit. This will bring honor to my Father. I have loved you as the Father has loved me. Now continue in my love. I have obeyed my Father's commands, and he continues to love me. In the same way, if you obey my commands, I will continue to love you. I have told you these things so that you can have the true happiness that I have. I want you to be completely happy." John 15:7-11 ERV

A calm feeling that she had not felt in a very long time came over her. At that moment, she knew that the love God had for her would transcend any mistakes she had made. She needed to repent, turn from this, and ask for His help. He loved her, and she could feel his presence. The thought came softly and unprompted. She would call the church she had been attending and explain her dilemma to whoever answered the phone. She desperately needed direction, and the church was an excellent place to start. Janice was determined to take complete charge of her life now, so she got the phone number and dialed it. There was no time to be fearful, embarrassed, or ashamed.

A kind voice answered the phone at the church and identified herself as Mrs. Alice Donaldson. Janice began, "I am a student, and I have been attending your church while I am here in school at the University." Without hesitation and through tears, Janice poured out her story. Starting at the very beginning, she recounted every detail of her situation. She recounted her original dream, how she met Jason, and the enervated moment when she became sexually active. Her fear was that she would lose him if she did not comply, and she also feared that she would lose the chance for a happy family with love. She explained her coming to a school that did not offer her major to obtain his promise of early marriage, and lastly, her living arrangement with Jason and the predicament in which she currently found herself. She told her how they had deceived both of their parents and how going back home was not an option for her. She feared that she would not be able to finish the uncut version of her story, so she did not give the woman on the other end of the line a chance to speak. She pushed forward with her sordid tale as much for her emotional release as for the voice on the other end of the line to hear it.

Alice Donaldson worked part-time at the church as a

volunteer for many years. She was a widow who retired from the United States Postal Service. She was proud of the work she did there. Her late husband and his family were lifetime members of the First Congregational Church, and when she married Harold Donaldson, it became her place of worship and service as well. Harold Donaldson served as a faithful Trustee and dedicated member. Mrs. Donaldson filled her days volunteering here and doing whatever small jobs they needed extra hands to complete. She taught young adults in Sunday school on Sunday and developed a special love for them. Several of them were college students who were away from home and looked to her as a surrogate mother. She listened to their problems, counseled them on their love lives, and helped them investigate internships and resolve housing issues. Mrs. Donaldson loved this portion of her volunteerism the most, the times when she helped guide young lives in positive directions that aided their passage to successful futures. Several former college students returned to her later in their lives and expressed gratitude for her role in their success. The students who expressed how much she helped them made her volunteer hours worth every minute. She did not usually answer the phone, but she happened to be in the office when the phone rang the day Janice called. The secretary left the room for a moment, so she answered the phone to relieve her.

The person on the other end of the line identified herself as Janice. Her voice was low and timid, and she spoke without waiting for Mrs. Donaldson to quiz her on the nature of her call. The voice on the line began to blurt out her reason for the call. Alice Donaldson decided that it was best not to interrupt her because she could tell that the girl on the line was emotionally distraught, and this was just not the right moment for a "hold while I transfer you" comment. After Janice got to the end of her story, the kind voice on the other end of the phone answered, "What do you want to happen at this point? God is a forgiving God who is ready to forgive you.

He has been waiting for you to choose to change your life." She went on to explain, "Sex is a spiritual and physical connection to another person created for a marriage covenant relationship. As a part of what God created for us, it should be a guilt-free experience. Although practiced outside of marriage, it can have long-lasting, unpleasant effects." Relieved, Janice assured her that she wanted to try to mend her life and lifestyle. Mrs. Donaldson prayed with her and got down to business. "Just give me a few minutes to make some calls, and I will call you back," she said.

Janice hung up the phone and felt the love of God as it overshadowed her. She started to move around the apartment, gathering the rest of her things to put into her car. Mrs. Donaldson had not made any promises, but Janice knew she would help her all she could. In the circumstance that she now found herself, even if she had to go home and face the truth, she was ready to do it.

It was good to feel free to tell someone the whole truth about her life. Until now, she and Jason were the only ones who knew, and perhaps her friend Sharon who let her stay over sometimes when the Millers came to town. Surprisingly, she realized she was humming a tune as she put her things into her car. She thought of another friend on campus that she had stayed with before. She knew it would be okay to come today, even without notice. No worries, she had enough left in her savings to get a hotel room for one night if she had to; all she would do now was pack and sing praises to her God.

Something in her heart had changed. Janice instinctively knew that she was not only packing her things to hide them; this time, she was also moving them from this apartment for the last time. She did not know what was ahead of her, but she knew that she would not be coming back this time. It was strange, but the thought made her smile and lifted her spirits. Suddenly her future felt bright again! After a few hours, Janice had removed any hint that she ever lived in Jason's apartment. She took a final look to double-check. There was not one single item left of hers in the apartment. Amazingly, Jason had not called to check on her one time. It was oddly liberating, empowering, and sad at the same time. It all seemed hopeless whenever she had secretly wondered how she could change her situation. Even if she decided to change her life and lifestyle, stuck in a strange city, she had no financial resources. Yet now, without any influx of money, she decided to endure whatever consequences she faced to never be in this predicament again.

Just as she put the last item in her car, her phone rang. It was Mrs. Donaldson; she had found a family in the church who housed college students during the year. They had a vacant room and were excited about meeting Janice and accepting her into their home. She could stay indefinitely and have as much time as she needed, even until she reached graduation if that was what she needed. Janice could not believe the favor of God that she was receiving. He had heard her heart and had provided the answer to her prayer. Elated, she quickly accepted but cautiously explained that she could not pay much. Mrs. Donaldson explained that this family was taking her in at no charge. After they heard her story, they wanted to help in any way they could. Mrs. Donaldson asked Janice to meet her at the church around five o'clock. Janice wrote Jason a short note that she would not be returning, put the key on the table, and closed the door to that chapter of her life.

She sang as she drove away:

> *Great is Thy faithfulness!*
> *Great is Thy faithfulness!*
> *Morning by morning, new mercies I see.*

All I have needed Thy hand hath provided,
Great is Thy faithfulness, Lord, unto me!

Starting Over

At five o'clock sharp, Janice drove up to the church. It was a massive building with beautiful stained-glass windows that covered an entire block. She had attended the church her first semester but had only come sparingly during this semester. The pressure she was under at home had drained much of her energy. Regrettably, she left off going to church, which she now knew was the very thing that would have strengthened her. Because it was a weekday when Janice reached the front entrance, she rang the doorbell she found labeled *Office*. She was anxiously waiting when Mrs. Donaldson's voice came over the speaker on the door. "May I help you?" she asked. "It's Janice; I spoke to you over the phone earlier today," she replied hesitantly. Suddenly, warmness came into the voice on the intercom, "I'll be right there." In just a few minutes, Mrs. Donaldson opened the door and gave Janice a warm hug. She had her purse in her hand already, and stepping out of the door she announced, "You can follow me in your car over to the Brockington's home. They are expecting you." Janice obediently made her way to her car and slid behind the wheel, grateful that she did not have to talk about her situation anymore. They drove off, heading to a place Janice could not have imagined would be open to her. She decided to trust Mrs. Donaldson and made up her mind that whatever the condition of the house, she would stay until she could do better. Her time in the neighborhood they moved to after her parents' divorce taught her to survive with less. She was walking in faith, not knowing what she would encounter next but trusting that God's guiding hand was with her.

Janice had mixed emotions; she felt apprehensive, greatly

relieved, some anxiousness, and oddly enough, hopeful. She wondered if she could get her life back on track and recover what she lost. At least now, it was a possibility. She did not realize how much she had suppressed her feelings about her new lifestyle. She had not let herself think about it for a long time. Now that she had allowed herself to think about it, she had been unhappy with her living arrangement from the beginning. She had become the woman Jason was hiding, not the great love of his life that made him proud.

John and Emily Brockington were members of the First Congregational Church, where Janice called the day of her crisis. They were both ardent worshipers who had been members of the congregation since their college days. They met at the church while they were students, fell in love, and got married shortly after their graduation. John pursued a career in Graphic Design, while Emily chose a career as an elementary school teacher. Their only daughter, Ashley, lived less than one hundred miles away, and they saw her often. At the beginning of their marriage, they wanted a house filled with children; however, that did not materialize, and they were thankful that they did have one daughter to love.

After Ashley finished college and took a job in another city, John and Emily started the practice of housing college students who somehow missed the housing deadline at BSU. Sometimes they were exchange students or students who needed help to afford student housing while not living on campus. They registered with the school as one of the alternative housing choices for students. Some students preferred a home environment while attending college rather than a dormitory or roommate experience. Either way, taking in college students meant more to them than to the students. Each student they housed made the house come alive with laughter and life. Although they did not have the blessing of as many children as they wanted, this was a way of parenting as an alternative. They lived in a large home, and when the college experienced overflowing enrollment, they often housed as many as two freshmen students until school housing could accommodate them or for as long as they were needed. After hearing of Janice's dilemma, they heartily agreed to help her.

Presently, Janice and Mrs. Donaldson drove up to a beautiful, well-kept, two-story home in a large, well-manicured subdivision. John and Emily Brockington answered the door, greeted them with smiles, and invited them inside. At first glance, it was a beautifully decorated, neat, and tidy home with an open floor plan, which was extremely spacious with modern decor. Janice could immediately tell that a lot of thought went into decorating this home. There were beautiful earth tones blended throughout the house from one room to the next. The entire rear wall of the combined kitchen and family room was comprised of floor-to-ceiling glass doors.

They all went into the family room of the home, where Mrs. Donaldson properly introduced them to each other; Janice felt at home right away. John Brockington explained that their only daughter lived in another town. When she lived at home, they created a small loft on the upper floor that consisted of two bedrooms with a sitting area between them, he was sure it would be comfortable for studying, and each room had a desk and private bath. They explained that sometimes, they housed college students intermittently for short-term stays when the dorms were overcrowded. They were both delighted when Mrs. Donaldson called them about the possibility of a student with an immediate need for housing. Emily Brockington confided that she had been feeling a little lonely lately with no students in their home, and she was happy for someone to fuss over. Mrs. Donaldson excused herself, saying she had to get home. She embraced Janice and told her goodbye.

At dinner, Janice talked with her new rescuers, and they became better acquainted. They were a kind and loving couple who made Janice feel at home. She smiled to herself as the Brockingtons helped move her things in and then showed her the rest of their house. They explained where everything was kept and invited her to feel as though she were at home.

She called her mother later that night and told her that she had moved in with a family from the church whose daughter had married and moved away. It felt good; until now, she had been lying to her mother about where she lived. When Mrs. Burns became inquisitive as to why she moved, Janice replied, "Oh, I ran into some problems that I will tell you about later, Mom." Telling the truth was so much easier than the lie she had been living. It was God who rescued her; she just knew it. Janice was starting a new chapter in her life. She slept soundly on her first night there. Her heart ached a little over the loss of Jason, but she knew that this was the best thing for them both. She slept with a peace that evaded her for a long time; she could not believe her blessing. She knew God was easing the hurt of the experience she was leaving behind.

After settling into her new environment that first night, Janice felt inspired. She spent the rest of the weekend online, researching her original college choice again. Would it be too much to hope she could turn her life around completely? God had brought her this far, and she had the faith she needed to regain her momentum and get back on target. She reacquainted herself with everything about the school again. She wanted to know if they would accept the work she had done at this university. She wrote down the numbers of all the departments she would need to talk with; it was like seeing an old friend again. This time though, she faced her challenge as an experienced Janice. One who had not only begun her college experience and understood the routines and what living away from home felt like, but if it were possible, she faced it with more tenacity and courage than ever.

Back to Reality

It was Monday morning more quickly than she wanted it to be. She had skipped going to her Friday morning class because it was one of the classes she took with Jason. The weekend had passed all too quickly, and Janice had let herself enjoy her new freedom from a suffocating lifestyle in the beautiful home into which she had just moved. She and the Brockingtons attended church on Sunday, and Mrs. Brockington had prepared a wonderful dinner that afternoon. She spent Sunday evening studying for a test she had to take the next day.

Janice left home on Monday, knowing it was time to face her life head-on. Over the weekend, she had been able to immerse herself in moving, unpacking, and planning her next move. Jason had left her at least 45 messages. By now, he knew she had not stayed with Sharon and wanted to know, almost demanded to know, where she was staying. She refused to answer his calls but sent him a text to say she was okay. She decided to turn her phone completely off because it was difficult to ignore his calls. Janice did not want to take the chance that he would be able to sweet-talk her into coming back. She felt strong, but she was isolated and in new surroundings. It had not been easy, but she had been able to channel her thoughts away from Jason. She used her time looking forward.

She needed the time to pray, think, and plan. Her greatest desire, at that moment, was to get in touch with the old Janice. The person she was before she met Jason. She wanted to remember the old Janice, who had unlimited hope and worked hard to create a great future. She wanted to reconnect with the version of herself who prayed to God for guidance. She did not want to talk to Jason, who, by reading his text messages, was repentant and ready to reconcile. She wanted to spend some time with God so that He could strengthen her before facing Jason's issues.

This morning, however, she would see him as their very first class was together. She braced herself as she started her car. "God give me strength," she whispered as she drove toward campus. Driving to the campus, Janice thought of her feelings for Jason. She loved him... or did she? Was this love, or were her feelings an outgrowth of her neediness for love? Did she cling to him because she needed to feel accepted and special? Right then, she knew she would have to find a real definition of love. She understood that strong affection was the feeling she had for Jason, but what is love? Her mind went to the scripture in 1 Corinthians 13:

Love is patient.
Love is kind.
It does not envy.
It does not boast.
It is not proud.
It does not dishonor others.
It is not self-seeking.
It is not easily angered.
It keeps no record of wrongs.
Love does not delight in evil,
but rejoices with the truth.
It always protects, always trusts,
Always hopes always perseveres.
Love never fails.

Based on that definition, she knew that she loved Jason. She also realized that she had given up too much to follow him. Janice realized that so many of Jason's actions did not fit the Bible's definition of love. He had talked her out of her strategy to satisfy his feelings. He was able to persuade her to lie to her parents, and his, and most of the inconvenience of the relationship was on her shoulders. She thoroughly examined all the ensuing events in minute detail as she rode to the campus.

She arrived on campus on time, gathered her bookbag, slowly locked her car, and headed to class. Each step brought a greater sense of dread to her. What would Jason say? How would she react? She could not wholly disconnect from him in such a short time. It had only been a weekend, and their relationship was one of cohabitating, during which she dreamed of spending the rest of her life with him. She was almost at their class. There was not much time left before she arrived. She spoke quickly into her phone: "Give me the definition of love from the Bible." The phone searched the internet, and the answer came back:

The primary meaning of the word "love" in Scripture is "A purposeful commitment to sacrificial action for another." bible-truth.org/msg38.html

After Janice read the definition, she knew she would have to face the fact that Jason did not fit either of the definitions for love that were from faith-based sources. They were definitions that she trusted because they did not depend on feelings that could change. She put her phone on silent, quickened her step, and moved swiftly to class. Jason's face was the first thing she saw entering the class.

He did not have his usual confident smile and charming look but rather a sad, pitiful, repentant look. "Be strong," Janice repeated to herself again as she took her usual seat next to him. "Good Morning Jason," Janice said slightly too loud. She smiled and turned her attention to their instructor, who was giving their assignment instructions. It was difficult not to notice if Jason answered. All she could do was keep her eyes forward. There was definitely a long discussion about to occur after class. "Lord give me strength," Janice whispered again as she reaffirmed her resolve not to tell him where she was staying. Since he did not go to church, there was no other way for him to find out that she had turned to the church for help. The instructor droned on with the lecture, but Janice was in deep thought. After her conversation with Jason, Janice concluded that she would change her phone number. She did not want to leave a breadcrumb trail for him to find his way to her. She also knew she needed to remove the temptation to answer his calls from her day-to-day movements.

It was not her desire to hurt or be cruel to him. However, she did not want to risk his persuading her to go back into the situation from which God had rescued her. Janice remembered what her mother said to her, "If Jason loves you now, he will love you if you follow your dreams." Somehow, Janice doubted if Jason would still be waiting for her after she left this place to pursue her education in another city apart from him. It was probably the end of their time together. She had gotten to know him all too well. If he could not be faithful to her when he had to come home to her every day, he probably could not accomplish it with her living in another state. No, it was time to take a closer look at the information that was right before her.

The Danger of Not Believing What You See

Janice saw many things about Jason during their time dating. When they were in high school, she saw that he was slow to finish his assignments, and when he did do his assignments, it was not his best, but just enough to get by. She knew that he overslept the day of the SAT. Jason impressed Janice so much with his talk about college that she just glossed over the fact that his performance in high school was a signal that he would not be a good college student. She ignored the fact that Jason was lazy. His laziness would not magically go away. Jason was a lazy boy who would become an even lazier man. She even saw his rude, aloof behavior, but he showed love for her, so she excused his behavior toward others. He was under too much pressure from his parents was her excuse for that. Even though he spent his days after school playing video games and napping, she placed the blame on his parents for expecting too much. She refused to believe Jason's ex-girlfriend's stories about his poor treatment of her. She believed Jason's side of the story without even considering the other side. Janice did not contemplate that one day she would be on the receiving end of his rude, unfriendly attitude.

During those days, she was the object of his attention. She overlooked the fact that the pressure his parents were putting on him was to do the right thing or that it was only pressure because he refused to comply. When Jason pressured her to be sexually active, even though it went against the moral and religious standards she set for herself, she convinced herself that it was because he loved her. When he was willing to sabotage her ambitions, she reasoned it was because he wanted to deepen their relationship and was looking at their future together.

She prepared to talk to Jason after class. She hardly heard the professor or the lesson. She reasoned with herself, "I must face the whole truth about my situation and how I got here in the first place to gather the strength to propel myself forward." Jason had talked her into moving into the apartment with him to satisfy himself and his needs, not to plan their future together.

Janice could not ignore, however, that she had been a willing participant. She was unwilling to stand up for what she believed to hold on to him. Janice felt used and cheated but then stopped herself mid-thought to remind herself that she had agreed to this arrangement. She had been a willing co-conspirator in this mess. It felt as though a light was coming on in her mind, and she could see more clearly than ever things that she never saw from this new perspective. She must now also face her role in this catastrophe. Not all the blame lay on Jason; she merely had been making excuses for anything in their relationship that made her uneasy. She had agreed to compromise what she believed for the sake of love. Jason did not alter her plans; she decided to change directions herself. The fault, she decided, must lie squarely with her.

The Bible taught that the truth would make her free. Janice knew that to remain free, she had to look past her feelings for Jason to understand why she made those choices. Facing the truth was necessary for her to make a new start that was stable and free of blame and guilt. She had to acknowledge her role in creating this problem in order not to repeat her mistake. In order to learn from her mistakes, forgiving herself was necessary. Then it was also necessary to love herself enough to pick up her life with perseverance and a renewed tenacity. She was brooding over these thoughts when she heard the professor say, "Class dismissed." Janice summoned the most courage she could and rose from her seat determined, resolute, and not to be dissuaded. She had faced herself and the results of her decisions; now it was time to face Jason.

Face to Face

Jason took his usual place beside Janice as they walked out of the door so that they ended up walking side by side. Jason was quiet; Janice broke the ice by saying cheerily, "Well, good morning again!" Her cheery greeting put him at ease, and without hesitation, he asked, "So when are you coming home?" His question came with the painful awareness of someone who knows they have messed up. He looked sorry, and he was sad. "Stick to your guns," Janice said to herself. Remember all the trouble that look has gotten you into already," she thought as she remembered the many times he had been sad and repentant before now. She knew it only lasted long enough to get her to do his bidding. She answered Jason softly, sidestepping his question. "Let's find a quiet place to sit and talk," Janice said.

Outside of the Fine Arts building where they attended class, there was a beautiful gazebo. It sat to the left of the structure in a well-kept grassy area designed for students to relax. It was large enough for ten people, comfortable, and a natural color of pinewood with seats built around its banister railing. Although it was a little chilly outside, they needed privacy to talk, so they walked silently over and sat down.

When they sat down, Jason said, "Look, I know I messed up asking you to move your things." Janice assumed he had already talked to his mother. I don't know why I did that, but I knew that you were angry, and right now, I only want you to come home." Janice waited patiently for him to bring up the girl he was with and the incident that occurred that fateful night; he never did. She watched him curiously as he talked, pouring out his heart about how lonely he felt during the weekend and professing his love for her. He missed his assignment that was due because he could not figure out the items for the project. Even in her hurt and dismay, she left everything for him to complete his project laid out on the table in the kitchen. She could not help but think, "He is doing it again. Jason is shifting responsibility for his actions and disregarding all that I must be feeling." She instinctively knew that for Jason, this moment was about him and his feelings. He was not apologizing; he was looking to regain the comfortable combination of girlfriend, tutor, house cleaner, and bed partner that made his life work. The moment they were having was not at all about her. How could she have been so blind?

She listened in silence to all he had to say. He did not even notice that the conversation was one-sided. She was glad that she had the time away from him to regain her spiritual balance. She listened to Jason this time from a different perspective. She paid attention to his willingness to compromise her life further to fix his. He made several promises, most of which she had heard before. He was ending now, "I believe God means for us to be together forever." That line usually worked for him, he reasoned.

Janice maintained her silence for a moment to reflect on all Jason had said and all she had felt before she spoke. Janice had played this moment repeatedly in her mind, and she was determined to make a clean break. To ensure Jason understood her and that her intentions were not lost, she began, "I spoke with your mom Friday morning; she said she would not be coming until spring." He looked uneasy and shifted in his seat. Without hesitating, she went on, "Since you insisted that I had to find a place for the weekend, I found one where I can stay permanently." His uneasy look changed to one of shock. She continued, "I did a lot of research during my spare time this weekend. I can transfer my time to Johnson State and not lose any of the credits I earned here. I will stay here until I can complete this semester, but I am considering not returning after the end of this term." She did not look into his eyes at this point because she had to get it all out; she did not want her emotions to betray her, so she plunged forward. "My new place is quite comfortable. I even think I can focus more on my classes from there."

Jason looked up; he seemed dismayed and genuinely hurt. He did not see this coming. He had taken for granted that Janice would forgive him as she usually did after a cooling-off period. Sure, he knew she would be angry, and he might have to grovel a bit, but he did not expect her to stay away permanently. He had always been able to change her mind. Jason felt confused and blindsided. Where did she get the money to stay somewhere else? She barely made enough to pay her car note. He knew she was not with Sharon; he had already checked. Until now, he had been the only person she knew well enough to move in with permanently. She did not have resources from home to get her a place alone, and he could not imagine that she really did have somewhere else to go. Was Sharon telling the truth? He knew she did not care for him. He also knew Sharon could only let her stay in the dorm for a few days at a time. He understood that he had to think fast to redeem this situation. He had never seen Janice so serious.

He began, "Jan, we're so good together, and I believe we should stay together. I believed we would get married after we finished here. (He knew that one always melted her heart) I know you want to get married too, but you know my parents, they won't stand for that now. I have been looking at engagement rings," he lied. I should not have gone to the diner with Amy, but she just kept nagging me to go. After you left the diner and I came home, I was just scared to talk to you about it because I knew you were mad at me. I thought if you went to Sharon's for the weekend, you would calm down, and I could explain," he was lying, but he was desperate. "Please come home." Janice listened intently, this time to what he was saying. There was no apology in what he said, there never was, and the promise of marriage was a carrot he had been dangling for a long time. Right now, she did not have an appetite for carrots! She realized while he was talking that she had not made herself blunt enough; he was not clear that she had absolutely no intention of moving back in with him.

"Jason," she started again, "I'm sorry, but our relationship has to end here today." She did not go into any further explanation about her decision which would have elicited more debate from him. Thus far, he was grasping at straws with his only intention being to get her back into his apartment. Janice believed his whole reason for wanting her back was for his security. She had made herself clear; she gathered her things, stood up, and told him goodbye.

Jason felt the finality in her words; he reasoned within himself that he would let her go now because she was still too angry. He started making plans to call and text her for a few days more; he knew her well. She just needed a more extended cooling-off period than he anticipated. He knew he had messed up big time. He sure was glad that she did not know the whole truth about Amy; he had her over to his place for the weekend, it was risky, but she was pressing him to see where he lived. Jan had grown accustomed to moving her things for his parents to come over; he thought it would be routine. If he had to choose between Jan and Amy, he would select Janice. Amy just wanted too much. She was a spoiled overachiever who required a lot of attention, and she did not know how to take no for an answer. Janice was much easier to live with; he could convince her to do almost anything. He was not too worried about her anger right now, she had been angry before, and he was able to turn her attitude around. He just needed to be more careful in the future. Now that Janice had a car, she could show up at any time. All the times he had done this before, she had been clueless. He just needed to get her back in place. His actions were a significant offense, so he would not push too hard. He would wait a few days and then re-approach her.

Jason felt sure that even though Janice had given her departure speech to him today, he knew he was always able to persuade her to do what he wanted. She loved him, and besides, her money would run out soon, and she would have no choice. She was primarily dependent on him. Her father certainly would not send the money to her. He was glad he had convinced her not to get a job that offered many hours; her lack of funds kept her reliant on him. Jason made his plan. He would call her tomorrow, he did not want to appear too anxious, and his next move was to bring a gift for her to class. With that taken care of, he was confident she would be home by the end of the week. He shrugged off the entire incident after Janice walked away, sure that she loved him. As for Amy, he would just put a little distance between them. He still liked her, but he wanted to live with Janice. With his plan in place, Jason went to find himself some lunch.

Janice walked away from their encounter with her heart aching. She forgave him as she walked away and prayed for God to bless him. This move was the right thing for her. With every step she took as she walked away, she felt God's hand as he began to restore her. He had given her time to evaluate her situation with clarity. He had also given her the courage and strength to leave. She was also required to go through the process of making the break for herself. God gave her the grace to do it. She thought to herself, "The next time I fall in love, I will follow God's road map. After all, it is all right there in the Book."

Sharon called Janice early Saturday morning. "Where are you?" She quizzed. "Jason has been calling me all weekend asking me about you. I would not give him a direct answer, but I also did not let him know that I do not even know where you are staying. Are you okay?" Sharon's voice was full of concern for her friend. Janice had intentionally not told Sharon where she was staying. She knew that Jason would call her first. "I'm okay; in fact, I'm great for the first time in a long time," Janice told her. I moved in with a family from the city. She was careful not to reveal too much. She did, however, want to calm Sharon's agitation about her well-being. Sharon calmed down, "So it's over with you and Jason, huh? I saw him around with Amy McGee this week. I wondered if that had anything to do with you not being around."

Sharon's words hit Janice like a blow to the stomach. She saw Jason in class only yesterday. He left a small gift on her desk in the class they shared on Wednesday and Friday mornings. He also invited her to have lunch with him every time he saw her, although she always refused his offer. It was their only communication since she stopped answering his calls. She did not want to hear about him and Amy. She had secretly hoped that her suspicions about them dating were not true. "There I go again," she thought, " not believing what I see." As it turned out, after all his talk about getting her back, Jason still saw Amy openly on campus, although somehow, he avoided being seen by her. He knew her movements too well. He knew which routes she would take to move about campus during the day. Janice returned her attention to the conversation that was still going on. Sharon was still talking. "Well, can I get your address?" Sharon was asking. "No, I think it's best for both of us if I keep this to myself for now. We can keep in touch by phone, and I will see you on campus. Perhaps we can have lunch next week." Sharon was quiet, so Janice broke the silence, "I'll call you early next week; thanks for checking on me." Janice hung up, knowing that she was leaving her friend in suspense but believing she was doing the right thing.

After she hung up, she sat quietly with the phone in her hand for a moment. There was no more denying it; she did not need to explore any other scenarios. Jason was still dating Amy. She suspected it, but it had been easier to believe that they were just friends, as he told her. It hurt her to think about it since this rang true to her. "Stop thinking about it," Janice thought. "God has given you a new start; keep moving forward," she told herself. "There is a bright future for you after this." She turned her attention to the chapters she needed to read for the next week. She had not read long before Mrs. Brockington called her to dinner. "Stay in the present moment," she thought to herself. "Do not let your thoughts drift."

Janice knew that rehearsing and repeating a situation in her thoughts served no purpose except to keep her sad. It would not help; it would not change anything. No, she had to keep her thoughts in the present moment. This situation will only stay alive if she keeps it on her mind. Her life was good; she was in a beautiful, safe environment. She completed the application to Johnson State, intending to transfer sooner rather than later. Now she was waiting for their acceptance response; her grades were excellent, and she was confident that they would admit her. She decided at that moment to leave the past in the past. The future was like a bright light shining in lots of darkness. She got up and went downstairs to dinner.

Jason tried to reach Janice repeatedly that week. He knew she was angry but felt that her anger would have subsided by now, and she should have been back with him. What other choice did she have with her small savings account balance? He took gifts to her for the last few days in classes they shared. That had always worked when she was angry. Janice's demeanor was pleasant and cordial, but she refused to discuss coming home. He wondered if Sharon had told her she saw him with Amy the other day. He was trying not to let Sharon get too close to them, taking Amy in the opposite direction. That encounter would require awkward introductions. He reasoned that even though Amy was not his first choice, he did not want to let her go until he knew Janice was returning to his apartment. If he had done that, he would have lost everything. Janice had always been amenable, but now she was cordial and distant as if they were just casual friends. Amy was brilliant, though, and she had helped him complete that project he had due after Janice left. He did get partial credit for the late work. Janice did not even care that she left him before she had a chance to explain her idea for his project. She knew it would put his grade in jeopardy. Jason thought that it was totally insensitive of her to take the chance that he might fail. He wondered if he could ever trust her again. She moved out permanently and would not say where she was living! She had not seemed concerned at all about the predicament her leaving had caused him. His mother would want to know why they broke up. Jan knew all of this. Frustrated, he picked up the phone and called Amy. He needed some help with his current assignment.

Reflective Questions

1. Can you forgive someone and dissolve your relationship with them?

2. What should you do if leaving someone means you will hurt them?

3. Are there signs in your life that are signaling you that it is time to turn around and change the path you are on?

Prayer

Heavenly Father, I come to you. I ask for the courage to make changes that I need to make to transition to a better life. Thank you for Your sufficient grace to enable me with the courage to move forward with confidence. I believe that you are watching over me.

Chapter 5
Rebound

...so that everyone that believes in Him would not be lost but have eternal life.   **John 3:16 ERV**

Personal failure should not stop you from making your way back to God. Because God places great value on you, He is waiting for you with open arms. The scripture teaches us that even the hairs of our heads are numbered. (Matt. 10:30-31) He loves you, is concerned about you, and He will guide you to a better life through His word.

What do you do when your life is all messed up, you are ashamed, you feel like quitting, and you have no idea how to fix it? There may be times when you feel like you cannot face anyone again, and you are afraid that no one will ever respect or care for you again. The answer to this dilemma is simple; run to the God who gave His Son to die for your sins and who loves you without reservation. He loves you deeply despite your failure and wants to restore you to freedom. There are moments of overwhelmingly significant moral failure where things appear to be so bad that nothing in this world, or at least in the world you know, can fix it. Remember this: God's love is ready and waiting to release you from any guilt and shame you may be feeling and help you repair any damage done to yourself and your reputation.

Janice has allowed herself to slip into a life of deceit and moral failure, going against everything she held to be her standard for life to satisfy another person's wishes. There may be times in your life when you are at a loss as to how you can correct what turns out to be an awful mistake. While Jesus died to pay for all our sins, facing family and friends can often be challenging while admitting that you have allowed yourself to be in this position. At this point, Janice cannot allow her feelings of embarrassment or her reluctance to be exposed to stop her from making the necessary changes to her life. It was essential for her to make significant changes to move her forward and propel her to the life that God planned for her to have, a life without self-reproach and embarrassment. Janice has renewed her relationship with God and is seeking Him for a change. The Bible offers a remedy for us when we realize we have failed.

Four simple steps to rebound from overwhelmingly significant failure are:

1. **Stop**

    So put everything evil out of your life: sexual sin, doing anything immoral, letting sinful thoughts control you, and wanting things that are wrong. **Colossians 3:5-6**

2. **Repent**

    So repent (change your mind and purpose); turn around and return [to God], that your sins may be erased (blotted out, wiped clean), that times of refreshing (of recovering from the effects of heat, of reviving with fresh air) may come from the presence of the Lord; **Acts 3:19**

3. **Forgive Yourself**

    Therefore, there is now no condemnation [no guilty verdict, no punishment] for those who are in Christ Jesus [who believe in Him as their personal Lord and Savior]. For the law of the Spirit of life [which is] in Christ Jesus [the law of our new being] has set you free ... **Romans 8:1-2**

4. Start Over

I say this because I know the plans that I have for you." This message is from the Lord. "I have good plans for you. I don't plan to hurt you. I plan to give you hope and a good future. Then you will call my name. You will come to me and pray to me, and I will listen to you. **Jeremiah 29:11-12**

Steps to Rebound

Stop

Will Rogers once said, "If you find yourself in a hole, stop digging." Paraphrasing his statement, "Whatever you are doing that has brought you to this impasse, just stop." Do not keep moving in the same direction, doing the same things, and thinking everything will change. If you feel that there is something unsafe about stopping or that someone will harm you, ask someone reliable for help. If it is an emotional entanglement, and you cannot find the strength to leave, ask God to help you. *"But ask the Lord Jesus Christ to help you live as you should, and don't make plans to enjoy evil."* **Romans 13:14**

You cannot recover from anything if you do not remove yourself from whatever problem has snagged you. No matter how deep the hole is that you dug for yourself, cease now from making it deeper. You may have to work your way free from the situation. Begin the process of moving carefully and safely away from what has entangled you. God is there to help you. Sometimes you may even need professional help to break free, but first, begin in your heart to move in God's direction. If a sudden stop will put you in physical danger, seek professional help. Go talk it out with someone who can either help you or point you in the right direction. Rid yourself of every excuse as to why you cannot get free and move toward your goals. He is always waiting for you to make Him your choice. Just make sure there is a steady progression toward freedom. You will find the help you need along the way, or maybe, all at once.

It may be a bad habit or a destructive relationship that has brought you to this place, neither of which you can be free of. First, you may have to rearrange your thinking processes or break away from the people, places, habits, and objects around you that bring temptation to your door. No matter what it takes, STOP. God's grace, which you cannot earn, but that he freely gives, is enough for you, and his strength can lift you when you are weak. God's grace can give you both the aspiration and the emotional capability to stop.

Repent

Turn away from whatever situation that has compromised you. The turn may be difficult but turn in your heart first, then follow through with action. Repentance begins in your heart; it is the process of acknowledging your failure and starting the practice of doing it another way. First, you must conclude that you are wrong and need to change what you are feeling or doing. The process of changing your situation can be challenging, but you can do it. Again, seek professional help if you are in a dangerous situation and need help to escape.

Change your actions and thoughts, or your life will stay the same. You will not get different results if you keep doing the same thing, nor will your life change if your thoughts remain the same. Sometimes you must take baby steps but take the step. Nothing will change if you do not intentionally target it. The Bible offers us a roadmap that will lead us the right way. It brings light to dark situations and provides hope for hopeless ones. The word "repent" itself means to "turn away from sin." Turn to God and a good Christian Counselor for help if you need one.

Forgive Yourself

Probably the hardest part of this process can be forgiving yourself and ending feelings of remorse and embarrassment. Once we confess our sins to God, He forgives us. The scripture says, *"...He will not stay angry with them forever, because he enjoys being kind. He will come back and comfort us again. He will throw all our sins into the deep sea."* **Micah 17:18-19**

A necessary step in your recovery is to forgive yourself. Forgiving yourself literally demands that you should stop looking at yourself in a negative light and stop thinking of yourself negatively. *"Look, the grief I experienced was for my benefit. You delivered me from the pit of oblivion. For you removed all my sins from your sight."* **Isaiah 38:17** The Bible makes it clear that God forgives us once we repent. There is no need to walk around feeling self-reproach and humiliation anymore. Move away from the people who want to view you from the context of your mistakes. God has countless other people that you can befriend. Do not hold on to people who make you feel small and diminish your worth. Live as though your slate is clean because it is!

Start Over and Re-Earn Trust

Sometimes in the wake of your recovery from a past mistake, there are damaged relationships, damaged from your actions, or lack thereof. If there are relationships that need mending or time that you must spend regaining the trust of others, be willing to submit yourself to the process. You must be willing to invest the time needed to do so. Most people will trust you again after a time of sustained good behavior. For those who do not, or refuse to forgive you, just remove yourself from their presence, not grudgingly, but in a kind and remorseful way. Once you have done all you can to mend the relationship and it becomes painfully clear that the person or people are not able or will not forgive you, respectfully move away from them and give them time to heal. Do not carry the burden of their lack of ability to forgive, which is their flaw that they must reconcile. Courageously and with the right mindset, forgive them and move on. You must only do what is right and respect yourself for having the courage to do it!

Five Positive Steps to Start Over:
1. **Start where you are** – acknowledge where you are in your development and start moving forward.

2. **Correct old behaviors** – develop positive habits and discard old destructive ways and thought patterns.

3. **Pray for guidance** – God's grace is there to help you as you surround yourself with positive Christian counselors.

4. **Apply the previous lessons that you learned** – Remember the lessons you learned on this journey, and do not repeat the same mistakes.

5. **Re-start your life with full, complete confidence** – Leave your past errors behind you and only use their memories to propel you to the next level of life. You are a winner because you have enough courage to change!

"So Jesus said to the Jews who believed in him, "If you continue to accept and obey my teaching, you are really my followers. You will know the truth, and the truth will make you free." **John 8:31-32**

Jesus says, "If you obey my teachings, then the truth you find in them will make you free." You can be free from your failure. You are free to start over, change, and transform into the person you really want to be. As you learn new things from his teaching and put those things into practice, you will find yourself becoming a person that makes you proud. If you accept it, you are justified by the price Jesus paid. It is a lot like someone who deliberately took something that did not belong to them, and another person steps up and pays the merchant for the stolen goods. The price of the goods is no longer due! The merchant is now appeased or satisfied, and you can walk away free of the incident with no remuneration. Jesus died on the cross to pay the price for our sins. He has justified us and made it, in God's eyes, just as if we never sinned. Jesus satisfied the price of our sins.

Christ had no sin, but God made him become sin so that in Christ we could be right with God. **2 Corinthians 5:21**

Jesus satisfied, appeased, conciliated, and disarmed sin to reconcile us to God so that we are able to gain God's favor. The anger of God towards us, as sinners, has been satisfied. Upon our acceptance of the marvelous gift, we are now in a position to be recreated in His image, transformed in our thought processes, and rehabilitated into people of God.

"Come to me all of you who are tired from the heavy burden you have been forced to carry. I will give you rest." **Matthew 11:28**

Reflective Questions

1. Do you need to stop and rebound from a personal mistake that is nagging you?

2. Have you been hesitant to walk away from a behavior or a person because you fear the results?

3. Can you believe the Lord's words and walk into a life free of condemnation and guilt?

Prayer

Father, I commit to you to do what is right. Thank you for forgiving me. Help me to put "old things" behind me and to reach towards all the good things that you have prepared for me.

Chapter 6
Renewal

Love never stops trusting.   **1 Corinthians 13:7 ERV**

God loves us, and he never stops trusting in our ability to decide to turn to Christ and start anew. His love for us is filled with acceptance and grace to assist in our renewed perspective and revived tenacity for life with *Him.*

When anyone is in Christ, it is a whole new world. The old things are gone; suddenly, everything is new!   **2 Corinthians 5:17**

The acceptance letter from Johnson State University finally came in the mail. Janice read the entire letter eagerly and carefully. She was accepted and eligible to register for the summer classes. The letter stated that a housing letter would arrive closer to the beginning of the semester. Janice was elated as she shared the news with Mrs. Brockington. They hugged and decided to go to a celebratory lunch.

Janice called her mother and told her the good news. She simplified the story and said that she was not happy at BSU and merely wanted to change schools. When all the arrangements were complete, she would be leaving BSU after her current semester. Her mother was happy to hear Janice so elated because it had been a while since she heard the excitement in her daughter's voice. She has worried about her ever since she decided to abandon her life's master plan to follow Jason to school. She knew how much Janice liked Jason, but Jason's demeanor caused her to feel uneasy. Janice had always brushed off her questions when she voiced her concerns and reassured her mother that she was okay. Even then, her mother felt that Janice seemed to be trying to convince herself, more than convincing her, that this was a good move. She prayed that Janice would get clarity about her relationship with Jason before it destroyed her future. She believed that she could rest now, knowing that Janice had made a good decision to follow her passion and not accept something less than what she wanted. Everything about this change in her life seemed right to Mrs. Burns.

It was the last few days of the semester at BSU, and Janice was unusually happy. She would be in North Carolina in just three weeks, living on her new campus! It had been a long time coming. Jason had stopped calling and was dating Amy full-time, and Janice heard through Sharon that Amy had moved into Jason's apartment. It felt strange to her at first because she felt that he made the decision a little too quickly, but Janice was able to make the emotional adjustment she needed to be okay with it. She felt a little sorry for Amy; "she should have asked me how her life was about to change," Janice smiled to herself. How much of her desires for her life would she have to surrender to Jason and his selfish definition of love? It appeared to Janice more and more as if Jason used women as a convenience. Amy was blissfully happy, never aware that although he had stopped calling, Jason was still trying to reconcile with Janice every time he saw her. As Janice observed, she thought, "Wow, this is what he was like even when I was with him; how many times had this happened that I never knew about?"

It was the end of the term, and Janice was facing finals and wanted to do the best she possibly could. When she transferred, she wanted her grades to represent her well. Therefore, she concentrated all her time on academics. It left precious little time for her to go over the details of her life with Jason. She was able to focus her attention on where she was going and not where she had been. When Jason occasionally tried to talk to her, she was always kind, and it was easier and easier to walk away from him. It was as if a cloud of smoke had dissipated, and she could see him clearly now. She was grateful for her freshly achieved independent thinking. She was thankful for the doors that had opened for her and felt rescued and valuable; at least she knew that she was precious to God.

Finals were over now, and Janice knew she had done well. At last, the day came when she packed her things into her car and drove away to a new life. Mr. and Mrs. Brockington helped her pack so that everything fit. There was no room for one more item to fit into her back seat or trunk. Mr. Brockington was very good at arranging and rearranging all her necessities into her car. They had bought her several items they knew she needed and even gave her some of their daughter's items left over from her time in college. What she could not cram into the car, they packaged to mail to her after she got settled. Mrs. Donaldson came by to see her off, and Mrs. Brockington prepared a wonderful lunch for them. Janice shared as much as she knew about where she was going and what would happen next with them over lunch, most of which Mrs. Brockington already knew because she had helped her to think through her next move. She thanked them for all they had done for her when she so desperately needed it. She explained to them how good it was for her to live in the Brockington's home, witness a loving relationship firsthand, and experience an environment where she was sheltered and not alone. They had provided a place for her to heal and gain new strength.

Living with the Brockingtons also gave her a picture of how truly functional homes really looked. They were a wonderful couple who were genuinely in love. They looked for ways to help each other and said, "I love you," often. Janice saw them make intentional arrangements to spend time together and not let their busyness get in the way of their time together. They were careful not to use angry words and openly discussed their different opinions with respect. They agreed to disagree on various topics, and if there was no reconciling of ideas, they tabled the issue for later discussion or not. Living with them gave Janice a new picture of a couple who loved one another. The Brockington's had a relationship that contained mutual respect. They listened to their partner's ideas and went about helping each other to achieve whatever endeavor they expressed. Janice developed a new mental template for love during her stay with them. It was more than a sensual attachment; it was an intentional effort to be a blessing to each other. They carefully fashioned and executed a mutual, reciprocal value of the other partner. Janice wanted to find that kind of love in her life someday.

She did not share with Jason that she would definitely not be returning to BSU during their talks. He knew from previous discussions that she wanted to leave, but he did not know that she was actively pursuing the move. As far as he was concerned, it was just something she said when she was angry. She did not want to chance him trying to talk her out of it. Without her prompting and help, he had not done well that semester; he failed one class and barely passed the others. She guessed that Amy was not being his Life Coach and doing half of his work as she had; smart girl! It was just like high school again; Jason was not willing to do the work to earn the grade, but this time his parents were not here to negotiate for him.

They talked in their last class together, said goodbye, and he promised that he would come by her house when they got back to their hometown. He proposed that maybe they could take a few classes together in the fall when they returned. Jason was not saying so, but he planned to win Janice back when they got home and discard Amy before the new term. By the end of one month with Amy, Jason had already decided that she would move out, and she would not be moving back in during the fall. She did not keep the apartment clean or cook like Janice. Amy was even messier than he was, and his apartment looked atrocious. Janice knew he still held out hope that he could change her mind about their relationship. They did not discuss it, but she heard that he and Amy were having problems. She did not ask him about it and was surprised that she really did not care!

Her farewell lunch was fantastic, partly because she was anticipating her trip. More than that, she was grateful to these two women who had rescued her and who were sharing their wisdom about life with her. She would forever cherish the gentle voice on the phone that spoke kindly to her and did not judge her when she called the church for help. No amount of money could ever repay the lessons about love and life she learned in the warm safety of the home that took her in. She was amazed at the God who provided a way of escape for her after she had made such a terrible mistake. For the first time in her life, Janice very clearly understood the meaning of the all-sufficient grace that comes from God. After lunch with the Brockingtons and Mrs. Donaldson, Janice got into her neatly packed car and headed to her future!

A New Day...

The first day on her new campus in North Carolina was exhilarating. She spent her first hours on campus settling into the dorm and met her new roommate Barbara who seemed nice enough. After not living in the dorm at BSU, this was a new experience. There was not enough money in her savings to get an apartment. Although she knew she would get a job soon, she did not want the pressure of a full-time life on her at this point. She had come here to complete her education in her chosen field. She spent the first day finding her new advisor and scheduling her classes. She toured the campus and found the buildings where she would have classes, visited the bookstore, purchased her books, and found the most important place, the cafeteria. She purchased the daily meal plan, which offered unlimited meals, as it was the most economical and seemed to be the easiest and cheapest route for her with meager funds. Janice sure hoped that the food was good, she had been eating Mrs. Brockington's cooking for her last months at BSU, and she was an excellent cook. Her first meal in the cafeteria told her that it was tolerable.

Before returning to the dorm that day, Janice had one more thing to check out. She drove to the church that Mrs. Donaldson recommended her to attend to ensure her spiritual life stayed on track. It was essential to make sure she knew exactly how to find the church. The car's GPS led her straight there, which was about seven miles from the school. Seven miles sounded like it was a reasonable distance away, but it was a short ride in her car. She got out of the car and checked the Marquis for service times. There was a service at 10:00 AM on Sunday, and they even had an outreach Bible study on her campus on Thursday at 7:00 PM. Janice pulled out her phone and took a picture of the service times, so she could refer to it in case she forgot. She knew that much of her success here would depend on her connecting herself to a local group of believers who shared her core values and views. When she completed everything on her to-do list, she went back to the dorm, relaxed, and finished reading a mystery novel she started reading last week. She wanted to complete it before classes began on Monday.

Janice got up extra early Monday, excited about attending her very first class. Jason called a couple of times during the weekend, but she ignored the calls. She knew he was probably just finding out that she would not be home for the summer. Although she resisted answering his calls, she had to admit it was not easy, even though she gained a measure of satisfaction from his pursuit. Her emotions about Jason were all over the place. One minute she wanted to talk to him and share all the adventures she was having, and the next minute she was so angry she could not stand the thought of him. Janice truly missed him a lot, but she was determined not to repeat the same mistake as before. She thought again about getting her number changed and quickly rejected the idea. All the people she knew had this number, and she did not want any of them to lose track of her or worry about her. She just had to resist answering Jason's calls. It was critical now for her to control her emotions. She could not open the door for him to sweet-talk her into returning to something she was so relieved to leave. Eventually, he would stop, she hoped.

Janice stepped out into the cool air early Monday morning, feeling as if the world was a great place again. She noticed that the birds were chirping, almost a melody. One would chirp, and the other would answer. Beautiful flowers bloomed along the well-manicured walkway as she listened to her footsteps as they carried her toward her destiny. She was grateful for the sound of her feet on this campus and was amazed at the many pieces that came together to get her there.

It was Jason's lack of attentiveness to his academics had prompted her to look for him on campus. Then she remembered the awful encounter when she located him at the diner with Amy. Jason then lied to her that his parents were coming to visit him. He had requested that she move out for the weekend, prompting her subsequent conversation with his mother, who revealed that she was not coming any time soon. She thought about Mrs. Donaldson, who had answered the phone at the church the day she called so desperate, and how kind and understanding she had been. Her mind turned to the Brockingtons, that had taken her in without asking her for anything. They treated her like family, almost as if she was their daughter. She thought of all the little seemingly isolated incidents that came together for her to make the transition to Johnson State. There had been bridge after bridge, blessing after blessing, to help her reclaim her life. Just at her lowest point, when she felt helpless, hopeless, and alone, her entire life turned around. God guided her to the necessary answers and solutions when she did not know where to turn. Now she realized that she must focus on her studies and heal from the pain of her losses. Her relationship with Jason had taken so much from her that she could never recover, but she would take the lessons she learned and do things differently in the future. Feeling sorry for herself was out; she was stronger, wiser, and more in tune with God than she had ever been.

Janice Reevaluates Her Life

A couple of weeks passed, and Janice was making new friends and loving her new life situation. She settled into her new church and immediately got involved with the different opportunities for serving that were available during her spare time. Every Sunday, she sat in the morning service and looked for principles she could and should apply to her life. She was enjoying the process of building a new Christ-centered life.

As Janice advanced toward her educational goals, she realized that if she wanted a well-balanced life, she would need not only to look at the things Jason had done but she needed to examine her motives and actions, as well. No one had forced her into any of those situations; she willingly took the course to bring her life to the disastrous mess it became. She had to reconcile the reasons why she allowed herself to rationalize every wrong move she made. Janice understood that her over-anxious desire for love had taken her life off track. Her family life caused her to feel overlooked; she had internalized it as a lack of love and based her life on those assumptions. The truth was that her family was in survival mode. They were all struggling to make sense of what life had thrust upon them. During the next few weeks and months, Janice analyzed her situation repeatedly. Although it was painful, she acknowledged that while her family situation was unfortunate, she had drawn those negative conclusions about how they felt about her. They had never expressed in any way that they did not love her. She even read articles on middle child syndrome to help her understand her feelings about her family. Janice knew that her mother loved her dearly, was very proud of her, had herself been a victim, and did the best she could to provide for them.

The ultimate, most crucial thing Janice had to do was forgive herself. She had repented to God a long time ago and clearly understood that He loved and had forgiven her. She had just never released herself from the guilt and foolhardiness of her actions. She did not think of it as not forgiving herself. She just kept asking herself how she could have been so stupid! How could she have gone all the way to BSU with Jason? Who lives with someone that makes her move her things every time someone comes to visit? How could she not have questioned why he was spending more and more time away from the apartment? The signs were all there; she did not accept it as her truth. If she kept replaying the scenario in her mind and feeling less than smart, it was a clear sign that she had not exonerated herself, which said that she had not fully accepted God's grace nor the full impact of Jesus' death for her sins.

Had Janice forgiven herself, she would be able to let go of the "that was stupid" feeling and realize that she is just human. It takes courage to start over and allow Christ to wipe the slate clean. One Sunday, she heard a message at church about the power of compassion and mercy. She had released Jason from responsibility for her decisions long ago. They were her decisions. This Sunday morning, the message spoke about how God was faithful and that He does not remember your sins.

Surely it was for my benefit that I suffered such anguish. In your love you kept me from the pit of destruction; you have put all my sins behind your back. **Isaiah 38:17**

Janice recognized that day that she was carrying a burden that she did not have to carry. In the next few days and months, she pushed away from the negative thoughts and replaced them with scriptures. Janice felt her burden as it lifted a little more every day. As the semesters turned into years, Janice went through the healing process that she knew was necessary if she was ever going to be able to love again without bitterness and resentment. She was now living with a heightened sense of self-esteem and understanding that because God loved her fully, even with her flaws, she was the apple of His eye. Memories of Jason paled into the background, and her feelings for him faded as she worked her way to total recovery. She did not have to look for love any way she could get it. She could let love find her. With her priorities properly aligned, she moved through her final years in college, completing each semester with honors.

Reflective Questions

1. Are you confident that God has forgiven any indiscretions you may have committed?

2. How sure are you that God loves you?

3. How willing are you to sacrifice comfort to gain your new start?

Prayer

Lord, thank you for watching over me as I evaluate my life with clarity. I consciously break from the people and things that would tie me to the old actions of my past and cloud my judgment. As I begin anew with Christ, help me to re-establish my life with all things new, new friends, new places to go, and new things to do.

CHAPTER 7
Restoration

Yes, you will suffer for a short time. But after that, God will make everything right. He will make you strong. He will support you and keep you from falling. He is the God who gives all grace. He chose you to share in his glory in Christ. That glory will continue forever.
1 Peter 5:10

Love Finds Janice

Volunteering at her church was restorative for Janice; it made her feel as if she was giving back to God some of what He gave to her. The church had been the safe haven for her when she needed help, and this was her chance to position herself to rescue someone else. It was wonderful not to feel burdened about her lifestyle and be free to worship, study, and have nothing to hide. She was no longer trying to be a model of someone else's idea of who she should be. She was progressing well, pursuing her inner passions for a career, and it felt good. Janice regularly volunteered at the church she attended when she first came to town. It was therapeutic to keep herself busy doing positive things when she was not in class or studying. She especially gravitated toward the children's ministry. They were so young, innocent, and unmarred by the world. She sometimes wished that she had the opportunity when she was a child to stay unspoiled and had the chance for the mentorship to which these children were exposed. Janice found herself content in a way that she had not been since the innocence of her early childhood.

With all the time she was spending at church, she had little time to appreciate the fact that she had transformed, and her view of being loved had too. It started with, and was enhanced by, her decision to stay in a Christian home, then understanding God's love for her had utterly overhauled her idea of what the word love meant.

Martin Howard

Janice met Martin while volunteering in the church's children's ministry. Martin Howard had joined the First Congregational Church when he accepted a job in Clayton shortly after graduating from college in Chicago. He was originally from North Carolina but chose not to return to his hometown of Goldsboro. His family thought that he could find a job nearer to their home, but he liked the position he found and the worship center he attended, so he decided to stay. After attending Congregational for a short time, he got involved with mentoring children; it was something he loved. He had experienced having a wonderful mentor during his teen years who helped to shape his life, so he wanted to help another child make sound and solid decisions using instruction and advice.

Martin also experienced disappointment in a previous relationship. He had fallen in love with his college sweetheart, Alexis Graham, who possessed the attributes he was looking for in a mate. Martin met Alexis at the student center a couple of weeks into his first semester. He developed a habit of going there in the afternoon after he got out of class to hang out. He noticed her right away but was apprehensive about approaching her. A couple of times, he was able to say a few words to her, which never turned into a real conversation. It was not until one of his friends came to the center who knew her and introduced them that he had his first real conversation with Alexis. They sat around all afternoon, talking and laughing. When his friend left, Martin offered to walk Alexis to her dorm. She agreed, and before he left her for the evening, he managed to ask her out again. They quickly became an item and were together constantly. They studied, went to games, and ate meals together. He absolutely adored her. She was bright and pretty with a quick wit that made him laugh a lot. Their relationship grew, and his love for her grew, as well.

It was not until they dated for over a year that he started to see another side to her personality. Her anger was explosive, and she became irrationally jealous. It was a gradual revelation of her dark side, and there had not been any signs of it before. He wondered how she could have hidden it for so long. It became as though she was obsessed with him. Martin did not find this flattering or acceptable. She followed him around, appearing in places they had not previously discussed, which made him feel like she was stalking him. Her anger was, in many cases, unreasonable, and her epic temper tantrums could last for hours. The potency of those episodes did not fit the minor disagreements that may have ignited her outbursts. Martin knew that although he loved her, he did not want to spend a lifetime with this kind of drama. So reluctantly, after many apologies and painful talks about how they could resolve their differences, he broke the relationship off.

The breakup with Alexis caused them both a lot of pain and anguish, but he knew that it was better to suffer now than to endure a lifetime of agony and unhappiness. It took him a long time to recover from the loss of her. He knew, though, that her last temper tantrum when they were a couple was the last temper tantrum he would ever tolerate. Although he had not given up on finding love for himself, he knew two things: The next time he entered a relationship, he would take his time and get to know the person before he committed his heart to her. He decided he would also take his time in making that choice. It was entirely too hard to have to disengage from a relationship that did not work. Secondly, he decided a pretty girl with a bad temper was not for him!

Martin noticed Janice in church service before he ever worked on a volunteer project with her. She was nice-looking enough and seemed to stay to herself a lot, but that was not what he found attractive. She seemed calm, serene, and happy. He wished he had paid that much attention to Alexis; she was gorgeous, but she never looked calm or content. Janice always came to service on time and left as soon as the service was over. There was never an opening for him to say anything to her, even though he looked for a reason to talk with her. He did not want to look like someone who trolls around to talk with pretty girls in the halls. He could not think of a line that did not sound made up and phony. Martin wondered about who she was and where she was from since she usually came alone. Occasionally, she would come with another girl who was not one of the usual attendees. She never came with a guy, and that encouraged him. After a couple of months, he even started watching for her when he came to church, hoping for an opportunity to sit next to her.

He got a little excited when they ended up volunteering on a project at the church together. He used it as an opportunity to engage with her in conversation and used every open moment to get close enough to talk to her. He prayed that she did not notice his anxiousness when they worked together. The more time they spent together, the more he liked her. After some time passed, he started sitting next to her in church. He did not want to appear to be a stalker, but he really did want to know her. Then it happened, they had a volunteer assignment together where he could ask for her phone number for a legitimate reason, but still, he hesitated. He did feel that as they worked together, he would have a better chance to get to know her and watch her interact with others. He thought about her a lot these days when he was alone.

Janice liked working on volunteer teams with Martin, who often served as team captain. He was intelligent, easy-going, and considerate. Sometimes she listened to the other female volunteers talking about him. They believed that he was quite a catch and took every occasion to be near him. From their conversations, she learned that he was single, had graduated from college, and had a great job. He was easy to talk to, tall and handsome. Janice often admired his work ethic and enjoyed her time working with him. He was fun, and his love for Christ was evident in his conversation and demeanor. She liked him a lot and thought of him as both charismatic and charming. The more she looked, the better she liked him. She found herself secretly hoping that they would work on assignments together. She was happy when they occasionally got to sit next to each other in church, which seemed to happen more and more often. It gave her a legitimate excuse to talk with him.

A couple of months before her graduation, they took the children from the church on a field trip to the aquatic center in a neighboring city. It was the most one-on-one time she had to spend with Martin, and they talked endlessly about their likes, dislikes, and visions for their lives. He was more relaxed and different on that trip than when they sat together in church. His manner was laid-back, and his conversation was amusing and interesting. She was surprised to know that many of their philosophies were similar at different points. Martin wanted a large family, and one of his greatest fears was to end up in a loveless home.

Martin felt free in their conversation that day and talked about Alexis, a girl he met in college and fell in love with, only to learn her personality was quite incompatible with his. His parents, who argued and fought a lot, separated early in his life. He did not want to repeat that situation. He explained that after his disastrous encounter with Alexis, he had delayed falling in love again because he wanted to get to know the person and not leap into a relationship that did not work out. He told her that he felt the need to have the ability to support a family. In his home, most of his parents' fights were about money or the lack of it. Eric, his father, believed his wife Jennifer was wasteful and spent too much on their children. On the other hand, Jennifer would say that she was doing her best; there was never enough money to cover everything. From Martin's point of view, in many ways, they were both right. His mother could have been a little thriftier, and his father could have investigated what the family needed and helped her budget. As it was, Martin said, "He gave her a certain amount of money and did not concern himself with any shortfalls except to criticize her spending habits." "They did not seem to be able to sit down together and reason through their differences. Perhaps they could have helped one another. Instead, they yelled and screamed at each other. They were both good people, but they continuously exchanged blame for the lack in their home," Martin sadly reminisced. Janice could feel the pain in his voice as he spoke of his parents' inability to reconcile their differences.

Martin's father, Eric, wanted to be able to influence his children in a way that his father had not done. He wanted them to be careful with money so that they could prosper. On the other hand, Jennifer was an only child who never had to think about money in that way. She did not understand his anger when she did what she believed was necessary for their children. They loved each other, but their differences drove them apart. Martin made up his mind at a very young age that he would not repeat the same mistakes in his marriage. He would have a peaceful home.

Janice shared with Martin that she was from a broken home and how she realized that her idea of love was inaccurate and faulty. She told him how her early images of love came from television. It was quite out of character for her to share how she allowed herself to believe Jason and how she had made excuses for his bad behavior instead of objectively interpreting what she saw. Janice told Martin how the Lord had provided her with an escape plan and delivered her. She did not know why she felt so free talking to him, but somehow, he made her feel at ease and safe enough to tell her story. She had not spoken to anyone about Jason since she left Biloxi, and somehow here she was, pouring out her story. God led her to a safe place to stay while she was in her crisis.

He was empathetic, assuring, and could almost feel her anguish as she spoke. He made her feel so at ease that it was almost calming, she thought. She had carried her story in her heart with no outlet and gleaned any knowledge she could from it while acknowledging that it had been a great mistake and not one she wished to repeat. After holding her feelings in so long, she was happy now that the hurt had subsided, and she could talk about all she endured. Janice also noticed that she did not feel as embarrassed about revealing her past as she thought she would feel. It surprised her that the shame and hurt that had been so strong was now little more than a memory.

After the field trip, as they waited for the last parents to pick up their children, he casually asked her if he could call her so that they could continue their conversation. She was stunned, but they had bonded so well on the bus that she felt drawn to him. She smiled easily and said yes, silently hoping he would call that same night. Driving home, she filled her thoughts with the day's events. Janice was afraid to allow herself to make too much of his wanting to call her. Maybe after hearing her story, he somehow felt sorry for her, poor Janice. She should not read too much into his request. What if his only reason to call was that after hearing how she lived with Jason, he thought she was a bad girl, an easy target? Janice wondered if she was overthinking this situation.

The encounter made her feel like a silly schoolgirl. She did not feel unsure or apprehensive when talking with Martin or sense that she had to measure up somehow to his expectations. With her entire story revealed, she wondered if it made him feel like she was used goods. "Do not bring your last experience into the present," she thought. "Learn from it, but do not build unnecessary walls to protect yourself." She and Martin had so much in common when it came to their ambitions and the things they wanted in life. She enjoyed their conversations and the way they shared their common goals. "Allow yourself to imagine a new, different future," she thought, "Trust God, and just be careful."

She understood now that she did not have much in common with Jason. The situation between them had been forced and was not in line with what she believed to be right. Most of what she wanted had to be forfeited while he had not given up any of his endeavors to accommodate her. She would not give up any of her undertakings again. "How silly," she laughed, "he only asked for my phone number; why am I making this into a romance?" She laughed aloud and completed her drive home, humming all the way. This time she would take the time to get to know him; she would build a friendship and evaluate any behavior he displayed. Janice chided herself for having such advanced thoughts about a relationship that had not even started and maybe never would. She had not felt like this for a long time. After her breakup with Jason, she had emotionally shut that part of her life down to focus entirely on her spiritual life and education. She could not afford to go off track again. Perhaps it was because graduation was near, her hard work and sacrifice were about to pay off, and she felt liberated and strangely free again. She had studied, applied herself, and paid her dues while in this new school environment. She moved with focus and determination. Now she would graduate with a bachelor's degree in a few weeks and be admitted to a Physician's Assistant Program. She earned top honors with her GPA and participation in on-campus activities. Only now was she open to new possibilities of what life could offer her?

She took her time that evening, putting things away and preparing to study for next week. Considering her room, she suddenly realized the space was very small, but she was grateful for all the peace she had there. She thought about the apartment she shared with Jason, which was spacious and had plenty of room in the closet. She smiled inside when she realized that this small room had offered her so much more contentment than she ever experienced in Jason's apartment. Now she was in her place and decided at that moment that from now on, she would consider her room to be snug and cozy, not a small space. Peace and contentment meant more than space to her.

With each item she put in place, she remembered when she had to move for the weekend when Jason's parents came to visit. She could still feel the humiliation and embarrassment it caused her. God had transformed her life and granted her heart's desire; all she had to do was be willing to make the change. She mused over how long she had allowed herself to stay trapped, hoping for an elusive marriage, feeling she had given up on who she truly was, only to have it restored to her. All the things she thought she had lost were there all the time. Attending the university about to receive her degree in the area that she initially chose was nothing short of a miracle. Janice felt so grateful.

It was later in the evening, after she had come from the dining hall and done laundry, that the phone rang. The voice on the other end of the line spoke; it was Martin. "Is this a good time?" he asked. "Yes, it is," as she tried to disguise the giddiness she felt. He called her! They talked for two hours before Janice realized how late it had become. He was so easy to talk to, and their interests were so similar. When she mentioned the time, he quickly said, "You'd better finish your homework; you are still a student for the next few weeks." Even those words made Janice feel warm inside; no one had ever cared about how much work she had to do or even if she got it all done. It just felt right.

Their conversation was about everything from their hometowns to where they hoped their careers would take them. They talked about the details of their individual enthusiasm for job advancement and opportunities that were available for their degree levels. It was amazing how strongly their fundamental beliefs matched and how much their future endeavors aligned. It was as though their movements were synchronized but in different lives. There were no selfish ambitions or unrealistic expectations. Janice hung up the phone, finished what she needed to study, and felt completely at peace that night after their conversation. She dressed for bed and went to sleep, still thinking about each thing they had discussed in detail.

It happened progressively. Martin and Janice started spending time together outside of their church volunteer work. They talked every day now and went to a few movies just as friends. He lived in an apartment, but they both agreed that when they spent time together, it would be in public places. Janice was grateful that she met someone who shared her core moral code. What impressed her most about him was that he showed so much interest in her viewpoints that he researched information and shared it with her. Her feelings for him were strong but not desperate. She liked it.

Their new relationship was taking its form as a genuine friendship with mutual respect for the other person's wants and needs. They built it on the solid foundation of regard for each other's hopes and desires for their lives. They prayed together over any issues that confronted them; there was no pressure on either side to challenge their spiritual walk to stay in the relationship. There was only a sincere desire for the other person to succeed. Was this the actual image of love for which she searched? Janice wondered. It was amazing that Martin agreed with her when she recommended only having dates in public places. They had been talking a couple of times every day now and had been out several times. Together, they agreed on abstinence until marriage. It took a lot of the apprehension out of dating again for Janice.

Because she had done so well in her program, Martin suggested that she pursue her PA degree right away. There were several paid positions available at local companies that she qualified for that he researched for her. She could support herself by working while attending classes. It would be demanding, but Martin pointed out that it would prove to be a valuable experience that would boost her salary long term. Janice had never been involved with anyone who took such an active interest in her career or who researched things that would be best for her. Generally, it had been the other way around; she was always looking out for others and making her way alone. Having someone to help was a new and refreshing change for her. Janice did not know where this would lead, but she knew she liked it. This time the person she chose to love did not fit her former prototype. He was a strong, affectionate Christian man who shared similar ideas, ethics, and love for God as she did. Martin was not emotionally distant as the previous men in her life were.

Jason Again

Then it happened. Just when Janice felt like her life was on track and she had met someone she was slowly getting close to, who shared her enthusiasm for life, Jason called. The phone rang, and without ever looking at the caller-ID, she just knew it was Martin, she answered. "Hello stranger," the voice on the other line said. Janice felt as if someone hit her with a brick. Why hadn't she checked caller-id before she answered? On the other end of the line was Jason. It had been so long since Jason called, and since she heard his voice, like a bad dream that you are trying to forget, she had stopped being worried that he would call. She stuttered an answer, "Oh, hi!" she attempted to sound cheery and tried to hide the disappointment in her voice. She believed it was Martin calling when the phone rang. The feelings that she had long ago put to rest stirred in her. "I heard that you are about to graduate; I would love to take you out to lunch to celebrate," Jason was saying. Janice ignored the invitation and said, "You should be about to graduate yourself; when is your big date?" She already knew the answer. Her mother had already told her that Jason dropped out of college and was working at the neighborhood pharmacy. "Well, I took a break, but I will be going back next semester. So, when will you be home?" Jason quizzed. "I am not sure when I will be home right now; it depends on what job opportunities present themselves," Janice said.

"I sure do miss you. I want to come out to visit you. What are your days off?" Jason quizzed. As though she had not heard what he said, Janice asked, "So when do you plan to go back to school? Did you give up your apartment? That was a great location." Jason's reply stunned her, "I gave up my apartment, but I was thinking of coming to school with you, did all of your credits transfer? Do you have a large enough apartment for a roommate?" Janice's heart went cold from fear, "Oh no, not here," she thought.

"That is too close for comfort."

She answered quickly, "No, I live in the dorm here, so there's no room for anyone." She ignored the question about the credits because all her credits had transferred to her new school, and she did not want him to know. Janice stuttered, "You may be better off returning to the same school since you are so close to the end. "He probably failed half of his classes without my support," she thought. "Well, I have to go now, Jason; it was nice of you to call." Without waiting for a reply, Janice said, "Goodbye." She could not muster the strength to repeat it, but she knew in her heart – this is over!

Feelings stirred in Janice that she forgot existed. Jason was familiar, and she had loved him. They had not broken up because she did not love him; they had broken up because with him, she violated most of her moral beliefs, her spiritual standings, and her educational goals, then he cheated. No, she thought, "I cannot return to something from which God has delivered me."

Even at that moment, she knew she could easily fall in love with Jason all over again. The things that drew her to him in the first place would draw her to him again. The other side of that was, she reasoned quickly, the things that caused her to leave him would also cause her to be unhappy a second time. She also knew he had once held a position of power in her life that enabled him to persuade her to do what even she believed was not best for her. With her mind clear and away from the situation, Janice realized that, like the story of Hansel and Gretel, she had left breadcrumbs for him to find her by not changing her phone number. She justified her choice by thinking there would be so many others that wouldn't be able to reach her. She needed to face the truth now, Janice surmised. She could have just texted her new number to the people that she wanted to find her. Subconsciously, she had kept this one tie to Jason. A number he knew well and could use to find her with ease.

Janice was startled as the Holy Spirit revealed this truth about herself. She had even convinced herself that her feelings for Jason were entirely gone. She was incredulous that she had developed a blind spot where Jason was concerned, but today when she heard his voice, old feelings had rushed to her. Shaken, she picked up her bible and read:

We have freedom now because Christ made us free. So, stand strong in that freedom. Don't go back into slavery again.

Galatians 5:1

The situation that trapped her had returned to trap her again. She read the scripture again and again. She felt Jason's return was an attempt to test her allegiance and dedication to what she had declared to herself earlier. It was an old bad habit knocking on her door to try her. Janice knew what she must do after her conversation with Jason; she called and changed her number immediately. God had blessed her too much, and she had come too far to return to something from which He had delivered her. The truth was that since she had left Jason, she had progressed tremendously towards her original goals. She was back on track with God, and her heart was open to true love. She met someone in Martin whose personality complimented her personality. He was as eager to help her become who she wanted to be as she was to help him in the same manner. No one had to prompt Martin to do what was right. He was committed to God and showed the same energy in everything he did. His motives were clear to her, and even though they had not entered a full-blown romance, there was great potential, and she did not want to take a chance at losing his attention. No, she thought. Jason had to go!

Reflective Questions

1. How important is it to recognize when an old habit or past entanglement returns to test your commitment to change?

2. How determined are you not to return to past people, places, ideas, or entanglements that could trap you again?

3. How can you protect yourself from returning to your past?

Prayer

Heavenly Father, you alone have saved me from my past. Help me to walk in the wisdom of your word.

CHAPTER 8
Breadcrumbs

The only temptations that you have are the same temptations that all people have. But you can trust God. He will not let you be tempted more than you can bear. But when you are tempted, God will also give you a way to escape that temptation. Then you will be able to endure it.
1 Corinthians 10:13

When God redeems our lives from failure, and we are moving in the direction of success, there usually comes a temptation to drag us back to where we were. We must resist any enticement to re-engage our past and confidently move ahead!

After Jason's call, Janice had to deal with her emotions leftover from her life with him. Somehow, she had just repressed her anguish and love for him, and now it was resurfacing and threatening her future. She was in a new place where she was thriving and making significant progress, she met Martin, and they were enjoying each other's company. She was not ready to say she was in "love" with him, but she certainly felt very strongly for him. Now that she had heard Jason's voice, it stirred other leftover feelings within her. Since his call, she had thought about Jason a lot and remembered the good things that were a part of their commitment to each other. They had entered a profound union of deception when they moved in together, and it was a covenant relationship without God's blessings. She understood now why God reserved that kind of connection for marriage. It was soul-affecting and went much deeper than feelings. Now she realized she was carrying baggage that had the potential to ruin her new opportunity for happiness. She had to think carefully and keep her head on straight because she was seeing Martin, and their relationship was blossoming. Her feelings for him were strong, and she believed they were growing into love. So, what was this that she felt when Jason called, and why did his call stir her so much? She concluded, "It was the remnants of an illicit covenant," one that was outside of God's design. She instinctively realized what she had to do, distance herself from those feelings and Jason.

Her thoughts were where she would start first. She had to stop allowing her thoughts to rest on Jason; she had to stop going over their conversation and his request to move in with her. It was not flattering that he believed that she was still an easy mark; it was an insult. She decided she would ask God to help her erase, or at least subdue, the emotions that still felt very much attached to Jason. She would forget what was behind her and reach for what was ahead of her. (Phil. 3:13-14) Before Janice was hope and a future; behind her was devastation. This time she would not repress the thoughts that threatened to captivate her mind and drag her back. She would acknowledge that those feelings were real and alive and ask God to help her manage, resolve, and put them into proper perspective. She loved her new life and could not risk losing it dealing with "leftover" feelings. She believed they would subside if she did not feed them by reminiscing and pining over Jason. She would not play the "what if" game. What if he's changed, and what if she had just given him a little more time? What would it be like if he did come to Johnson State? All of those thoughts were a bottomless pit that could consume her.

Martin now filled that role in her life, and he was a wonderful addition. There was no pressure from him to move faster than she wanted, and she loved it. She would not risk all the progress she had made with "feelings" that could drag her down to a place she did not want to be. It was weeks before graduation, and she was anticipating the moment she would hear her name called and walk across the stage to receive her degree with honors. Jason had no clue that she was this close to graduation, and she accelerated the number of hours she took and went year-round, which pushed her over the finish line ahead of schedule. More importantly, she and Martin were considered an inseparable couple now, and they were devoted to one another. He did not deserve to be involved in a Jason moment. She did decide that she would tell Martin about the call when she spoke with him to give him her new number. They were honest with each other up to that point; she did not want any deceit to creep in.

Graduation

Graduation week arrived, and Janice was overwhelmed with the prospect of completing this phase of her life without Jason in tow. She had submitted her graduation application, gone over her degree evaluation checklist with her advisor, picked up her cap and gown, and taken a picture in it. Janice was graduating with honors; her hard work and diligent study habits paid off. She received a job offer for a permanent position after graduation because of a recommendation from one of her professors. She had also investigated several Physician Assistant programs and had applied to many of them, one at a neighboring school. If the local school accepted her, she would stay in town to attend the program there. She loved the city she was in and had made many friends at school and church. Even if she accepted a program in another town, she and Martin had discussed how they could continue their relationship without a break. She needed money, of course, but she also wanted to give herself the best possible chance at success. The only thing left to do was pick up a simple black dress and shoes to wear under her cap and gown, and all her tasks would be completed for that great day.

Her conversation with Martin about Jason's call when she gave him her new number had gone better than she expected. It was a positive sign for their relationship that she trusted him enough to tell him the truth, and he was supportive of her decision to change her number rather than continually receive unwanted calls from Jason. He felt honored that she cared enough for him to close the door to her past. It also meant that her feelings for him were as strong as his feelings were for her. Her decision not to leave the city after graduation if they accepted her at the local medical college made him feel relieved. Of course, they would work their way through a brief separation if she had to go away, but his greatest hope was that she would not leave. Even if she went away to medical school, they agreed that she would not go back to her hometown afterward. She would make this town her permanent residence. It had become her home, and she was quite comfortable here; she made so many friends and acquired a great church family. Of course, Martin made sure that she believed he was worth her sticking around for pursuing a life together.

Janice, as she always had, did her due diligence, and investigated to find the most affordable, comfortable apartment in the safest neighborhood available to move into after graduation. No matter what happened, dormitory life had to come to an end. There had been replies from two of the PA schools, but word had yet to come from the local one she hoped to attend. Still, going home was not an option to be remotely considered, so she had to find a place to stay in the meantime. An apartment with a month-to-month rent schedule instead of a lease would be best until all the details were settled. After looking at 10 or 12 apartments, she found one that was clean, reasonably priced, and in a good neighborhood. She paid the deposit and was now busy planning how to decorate it. It was a one-bedroom, second-floor apartment with large rooms, and an alarm system, which was important to her. The apartment complex was new, was well landscaped, and its sky-blue siding with white trim was beautiful. Each building in the complex housed six units with parking for two cars. There was a decent-sized pool, fitness room, an ample laundry facility, and on the second floor of the rental office was a beautifully furnished clubhouse for tenant's use. Janice knew she could be happy here.

Janice had been saving for furniture, going to yard sales and thrift shops to find bargains for her new home. Martin was kind enough to store the larger items at his place since she was still living in the dorm. Her friend Bobbi was keeping some of the smaller items she found at her apartment. They spent several weekends laundering and pressing the linen and curtains that she found.

Janice opted not to send out invitations to many people back home for her graduation since she was so far away, but she did send out announcements to family and friends. They were simple and elegant on ivory cards with scriptwriting. Janice still had friends at home, but many of them had married and settled down with jobs and families. Some of them went to college, and she knew they would be happy for her, but she was out of contact with them now. She felt she only needed her mother and close family to attend. Her graduation was a family victory they all shared. Their family came through so much and weathered many storms. Now everyone was experiencing some level of achievement and victory, so they celebrated every milestone as a family success. However, she hesitated when considering extending an invitation to her father. They had not been very close since the family split. She finally resolved to do what was right and sent him an invitation as well. In some small way, she wanted him to know how well they had all survived, even without his help and support. Janice also wanted her mother to see that not all her sacrifices had been in vain. Although she was not able financially to send much from home, her mother had sent small care packages and sometimes even managed to send her clothes when she could. It would be the first time her mother had visited the campus.

Janice arranged for the best lodging she could afford for her. She was better off financially these days, but Janice wanted to give her this gift to thank her for being a great support to her. She was proud that she could do this for her mom. Her mother had given up so much to keep her children together. In her estimation, her moral responsibility was to give something back to her mother.

The first thing on her list was to take her mother on a tour of the campus and introduce her to her advisor. She would show her where she had been living, and it felt good not to have to hide her life from her mother anymore. They would attend church on Sunday morning before the graduation ceremony, and she would introduce her mother to Martin. They were almost inseparable these days, and she was hoping for a proposal any day. The hope mingled with doubt, even though they talked about it a lot. There was still the potential separation to consider if she had to leave town to attend a school somewhere else.

Mrs. Burns arrived on time on Friday morning, and she was so happy to see her daughter. Janice had not been home since she transferred here; these years had passed so quickly. It was expensive to travel, and she purposely did not want to run into Jason. Janice had to laugh at herself at that thought. She mentally went through all those changes to avoid Jason but left her cellphone number the same so that he could find her at any time. She was amazed at how she had not realized that this was why she had not changed it until the reality of it all hit her. "It is amazing how easily you can fool yourself," she thought. In some unconscious way, she wanted Jason to call. His call would validate her, boost her self-esteem, and somehow add some respectability to her past actions if she could feel he at least missed her from his life. It would help her feel as though she was not just a bed-warmer, homework helper, and housekeeper for him. That is how she felt in her low moments. He had let her go so easily, "hadn't he loved her at all?" she wondered. After that initial shock, when he called, Janice had honestly evaluated and cleared her heart of all feelings for Jason. It is funny sometimes how you cannot leave your past behind you unless you bring it into the open and acknowledge all those repressed feelings. Only then can you put them in the past where they belong, robbed of their power to influence you if they resurface. "The truth does make you free," Janice mused.

Janice took her mother to lunch and told her all about her goals and aspirations. Mrs. Burns listened intently. Janice had always been her child, who created a step-by-step plan of the ideas that came to her. It could be a simple project for school or some elaborate strategy she wanted to map out. She would fill notebooks with details, prices, and ways to accomplish her goals. Janice poised herself for success. Her meticulous personality would ensure that. She was proud and probably as enthused as Janice was about her future, maybe even more.

After lunch, they went to look at the apartment complex where she would live after she graduated and moved out of the dormitory. She was able to get the property manager to let her show a model apartment to her mom so that she could get the feel of it. Her lease did not start for another four days. The timing of her move worked perfectly because she had five days to move out of her room in the residence hall after graduation.

She told her mother all about Martin and their promising romance while they were touring the city, and they drove by Bobbi's for her to see the things they had chosen for her new apartment. Then there were the big pieces that she had been fortunate enough to find that were stored at Martin's. They would get a chance to meet tomorrow, Janice explained. The excitement of it all had them both in a great mood. Her mom started suggesting things she could send to help her fill her spaces. It was a delightful time for them both.

Then Janice turned the conversation to Jason and bravely told her mother the truth about living with him. She could see her mother flinch with surprise as she told her the details. She explained how she believed in the promise of marriage from Jason and how she had been disappointed. She ignored the changing expressions as her mother listened silently, letting her finish her story. Her expressions were registering first surprise and disbelief but then sadness that her child had endured this much disappointment and pain alone, pain with which she was all too familiar. Janice continued because she wanted to get it all out. She told her how she had to move out on the weekends when Jason's parents were coming to protect his image with them. Janice purposely left out Jason's cheating but did tell her how she called the church and how Mrs. Donaldson and the Brockingtons helped her. She tried to end her story with good news. She had sent Mrs. Donaldson and the Brockington's invitations to her graduation ceremony, and they both accepted. "You will get to meet all of them at the dinner I planned for everyone after the graduation ceremony," Janice told her mother.

Janice's mother's heart ached as she realized all the stress and pain her daughter had experienced. She regretted the fact that she had not been able to help her. She suspected that there was more to the story and that Janice was holding back to protect her. Jason's reputation for philandering since he moved back home had reached her ears. There had to be a catalytic event that caused the "big breakup." "Why didn't you tell me?" was her question. "I could have helped you; I love you, and I would never have let you suffer through that alone," she said. Janice replied, "I know that I should have told you, but I did not want you to worry. I prayed, and God delivered me just like he said he would, and look, Mom, I made it!" They hugged and held onto each other for a long time. Janice felt safe in her mother's arms. How could she have ever doubted that her mother loved her? The two women went to the residence hall, and after many, many introductions, they arrived at Janice's room where together they organized and packed Janice's belongings for her big move. Although it was not much work, it felt good that she had her mother with her to help instead of strangers. It felt good that she had confessed and that she could be completely transparent with her family about her life.

Reflective Questions

1. Was Janice reluctant to let go of her past, or was she secretly thinking she could shock Jason into changing?

2. Have you left a breadcrumb trail hoping someone will find you?

3. Why is it important to make a clean break when you leave a bad situation behind?

Prayer

Father, help me to be conscious of my motives and any hidden desires in my heart. Help me to be clear and transparent with my actions. Show me my shortcomings and give me the grace to make decisions and follow through with the actions I need to take for lasting change.

CHAPTER 9
The Wedding

"After you have suffered a little while, the God of all grace, who has called you to his eternal glory in Christ, will himself restore, confirm, strengthen, and establish you." **1 Peter 5:10**

It was at dinner after the graduation ceremony with her family, her father, the Brockingtons, and Mrs. Donaldson, that Martin proposed. Even Sharon had made it to her graduation. She was still at BSU with only one semester to complete to graduate herself. Janice called her to personally share her good news about completing her coursework and invited her. Sharon was happy to hear that Janice had crossed the finish line. There was no way, after all she witnessed Janice endure, that she would miss this celebration with her friend. This graduation was a triumphant moment in her friend's life, and she would be there to witness her happiness.

Her mother started by getting everyone's attention, giving a short congratulatory dialogue, then adding how proud she was of Janice and her accomplishments. After her mother finished, everyone at the table, starting with her sister, then her brothers, each gave their greetings and well wishes for her. Her siblings told anecdotes from their childhood with warm memories of good things they knew about her and her determination when she set a goal. Mr. and Mrs. Brockington talked about the blessing she was to them in the short time she lived in their home, while Mrs. Donaldson complimented her courage and commitment. Sharon talked about her courage under pressure and determined perseverance. Janice's father surprised her as he spoke of her tenacity as a little girl and expressed how he believed even then that she would be successful. His words surprised her because Janice always felt overlooked by her father and never knew that he noticed her at all. She felt a renewed love for her father as she accepted a new perspective for viewing him. It happened just after they completed their meal, and everyone was pleasantly chatting around the table.

When it was Martin's turn, he stood up, cleared his throat, and recounted how they met as he declared his love for her to the entire group. He spoke of how he noticed her at church and practically stalked her to find a way to sit next to her during Sunday morning services. Everyone laughed as he revealed the lengths he went to trying to win her affection. He talked about waiting around in the lobby until he saw her enter the sanctuary so the usher would seat them together. Martin told them how he finally got her number during a volunteer project and how he could hardly wait to call her. He spoke of her kindness and beautiful spirit. No one else may have noticed, but Janice could hear the nervousness in his voice. She had no clue why. She was so proud to have him there to show off to her family and friends. He was handsome and impressive looking. Then he turned to Janice, pulled the ring he purchased out of his pocket as he spoke, and asked her to marry him. She was shocked and disarmed at once. It surprised her; she had been hoping for a proposal in the near future, but her experience at BSU caused her to be afraid to allow herself to believe it would ever come. Her heart skipped a beat as she responded yes, right away.

There had not been any clues to her that he would do this today; they talked about marriage and their expectations with that kind of relationship. They even talked about the type of home they would live in "if" they were married. There was an unspoken agreement between them that they would marry someday. As it turned out before he proposed, earlier during this visit, Martin spoke with her mother privately about his intentions. He even took Mrs. Burns with him to make the final selection of an engagement ring while Janice ran last-minute errands for her upcoming ceremony.

Just before the dinner, as a gesture of respect, he also spoke with Janice's father about his plan to marry her. Martin was aware, from conversations with Janice, of the estrangement between Janice and Mr. Burns. He also understood that Janice loved her father and struggled with her feelings for him. Even though she genuinely adored him. Janice made it clear to Martin that she attributed all her rearing and nurturing to her mother, but he also knew that she loved and respected her father.

As a result of all he knew, Martin approached Mr. Burns before the dinner when he could find a few moments alone to speak with him. It was in stark contrast to his time with Mrs. Burns when he took her out to lunch and included her in choosing a ring for her daughter when Janice was busy with graduation rehearsal. He talked with her mother then and discussed, at length, his feelings for Janice and his intentions to ask her to share her life with him during the dinner. Mrs. Burns discussed Janice's need for love and security with him, which she knew all too well. She did not want to see her get hurt again. Martin revealed his background to Mrs. Burns and assured her that he was committed to Janice for life.

The proposal was something that Janice secretly wanted, but after her Jason experience, she was hesitant to hope for this moment. Janice's experience living with Jason caused her to wonder if any man was willing to abstain from sex until marriage. Then she met Martin, who was wholly dedicated to his faith and wanted the same thing that she did. It was an amazing blessing. She and Martin limited their alone time together to make sure they did not violate their abstinence agreement. Martin was a wholesome person who loved God and had strong ethical and spiritual standards. They had spent many hours together involved in volunteering at church and many other humanitarian projects. They talked for endless hours about the possibilities that their lives offered, and amazingly, Martin was a meticulous planner just like her. There were times when they disagreed. When they did disagree, though, they never said harsh things to each other. Because Martin shared his experience with Alexis, Janice was conscious not to let her temper get out of control. He knew of her "Jason" experience, so he handled her with care and concern, supporting her desires. The times when they found that mutual understanding was not possible, there was respect between them for the other person's difference of opinion. His proposal was like the answer to a prayer that even she was skeptical to believe could come true.

The acceptance letter finally came from the local medical college, which was a relief to Janice and Martin. He was already considering changing his job and moving if she had to leave. Now that they had a definite answer on which school she would attend, they could select a date for their wedding. They chose a wedding date six months later. The date would give Janice time to plan a small wedding and place the wedding date so that the apartment could be notified of her intent to vacate. The wedding would be held one week before the last day of the month. She could stay through her actual wedding day and have a week to complete her move-out and clean the apartment. Six months also gave them time to complete the premarital counseling their church required.

Premarital counseling included many subjects and issues that they might encounter as they vowed to live together forever. They learned problem-solving skills and anger management. They covered financial issues like spending, saving, giving, and they each had to bring a credit report to show the other. They worked through a conversation on physical intimacy, infidelity, and conflict resolution. Some of the topics in these sessions made them both squirm with embarrassment. The minister pressed on anyway, first forcing a conversation about Martin's relationship background and then hers. The counseling included an honest discussion on what annoyed them about each other and how much input each set of in-laws would be able to give. Those were some of the more difficult issues they covered, which opened the subjects they needed to discuss. They learned more about each other in those sessions than in all their time dating because it forced honest, open conversation. They discussed the embarrassing things that you never tell. The counselor had them discuss parenting styles and faith-based issues. By the time they got to how they would have fun together and its importance to their relationship, they felt as though they had been to marriage boot camp. Nothing remained hidden, and they were ready to join their lives with full disclosure and knowledge of one another.

Planning the wedding was challenging but fun. Because of Janice's attention to every single detail, and the planning tool she found online, there was not one thing left undone. Her sister came and spent the last week with her helping her to finalize every detail. The preparation and last-minute errands were a lot of fun, and they bonded again as sisters. They packed up her apartment in anticipation of her move to Martin's. Martin encouraged her to bring some of the furniture that she lovingly chose for herself just a few months earlier, and together they bought a few new pieces as well to make her feel more at home. They were mindful that of the principles they learned at the financial workshop they attended together, so they stuck with the modest budget they set.

Her mother came to town to help her pick the ideal wedding gown. They found it in the very first store where they stopped to shop. Mrs. Burns asked the clerk to put that dress on hold until they looked in several other stores, but Janice could not stop thinking about the first dress she had tried on. Her mother called an end to her shopping mania and directed her back to the first store when she realized that Janice was comparing every other dress she tried on to the first one. The dress was white, form-fitting, with a lace high neck collar and long lace sleeves. It was simply stunning, and Janice looked stunning in it. Mrs. Burns was overwhelmed with emotion when Janice appeared from the dressing room looking so beautiful.

Janice chose peach, ivory, and mint green for her colors. She and Martin decided to have the wedding and reception at First Congregational Church, where they first met. The church had a large social hall that could hold up to 350 people. That was more than ample space for their reception. An affordable caterer worked for the church's social hall. Janice had always been frugal, and excessiveness was not one of her shortcomings. She knew that, along with her mother and sister, they could decorate this hall and make it as beautiful as anything she pictured in her mind. She would use ivory linen tablecloths with alternating mint and peach table runners. They would dress the chairs in ivory coverlets with sashes coordinated to peach and mint green on the tables. Centerpieces would be tall Eiffel Tower vases with beautiful bouquets that featured peach, ivory, and mint green seasonal flowers, which a local florist would create. She would rent the Palms and other greenery from the same florist. They chose fine China, silver serving dishes, and a magnificent cake, which would be her main extravagance. Her sister found a florist that absolutely had the best palms and ferns that added the right amount of flora to the hundreds of flowers entwined with peach and green ribbon.

Janice chose to have an evening wedding, so she could use the street lamppost décor that she liked in the church. The six-foot street lanterns would line the center aisle of the church, draped with flowers and ribbon that would flow like streamers. The aisle would resemble a flower-lined street, complete with a satin runner as its base. The flower-lined aisle would culminate at the front of the church below a flower-covered arch. They would create the perfect atmosphere she wanted. Beneath the elaborate arch was where she and Martin would make their vows to each other and to God to love one another for the rest of their lives.

The flowers she chose to decorate the church and reception hall were just the right touch. Everywhere else, there would be Palms, Peace Lilies, and Boston Ferns. The flower girls would litter the white satin runner with peach peony petals for her ceremonial walk to Martin escorted by her father. It could not have turned out more perfectly. Candelabras flanked the beautifully decorated arch at the front of the church where she and Martin would stand. The subdued light from the street lanterns and the candelabras created the ambiance she desired.

Janice struggled with having her father walk her down the aisle. She believed that he had given up that right long ago when he left his family. Martin and her mother reasoned with her and convinced her it was the right thing to do. After all, forgiving is at the core of Christianity and its very base. By the wedding day, she had forgiven her father for their past relationship and believed they could enter a new relationship and leave the old one in the past.

She was thankful that she had invited her father to her graduation. He came, and they had the chance to begin reconciling their relationship. The two of them had dinner alone when he came to town, which gave them an opportunity to share their feelings. At that dinner, they talked through all that they each felt. Janice was surprised that she could understand some of his reasoning. She realized that she could empathize with a portion of his explanation, and it helped that she came to the table with an intentional, unequivocal, well thought out plan that this would be their reconciliation moment. She was thankful that she heard his side of the story but did not feel it resolved him of all responsibility for his children, no matter how he felt. Forgiving him had been one of the most challenging things she attempted in her Christian experience, but she knew that forgiving was fundamental to her life with God. She wanted her heart clear and free from any malice, so being angry with her father was a luxury that she could not afford. She understood that if she were to have a healthy view of herself and her husband, she would need to reconcile her past hurt that stemmed from abandonment by her father. After they talked, he told her he liked and respected Martin.

Janice waited, planned, and then she waited some more. Her wedding day finally arrived. It was indeed the happiest day she could remember! The wedding day started with thoughts of how God brought Martin into her life. She warmed with love for him as she remembered how they met and how much they had in common right from the beginning. Even as they planned their future, they designed it so that they both could experience the success and fulfillment of their goals along with those they had together. It was good that they had pre-marital counseling with their minister and had many talks about their expectations for life together. When they differed in their opinions, they found that with a little give and take, they could settle it. She understood now that love did not have to be one-sided at all. She learned that neither of them had to give up what they wanted for their lives to love the other. They could find a way to recognize, mutually, the value of unselfishly yielding to each other's wishes and sculpting new paths together.

She was in the dressing area of the church waiting for their wedding to start. It was a little unbelievable that the love she searched for so hard came to her when she gave up on the search. Janice was glad that she and Martin decided not to have the wedding in her hometown. It was appropriate that they were having the ceremony at the church where they first saw each other. Their families and friends did not mind traveling there to celebrate with them. They were facing a future with hope and awe-inspiring expectations because they had included God in their plans.

Present Day

Janice finished her coffee that morning after reflecting on her life and started cooking breakfast. Martin and the girls would be up soon, and they wanted to leave for church on time. They had been together more than 18 years now, and, if it were possible, she loved him more now than she did on her wedding day. Their marriage was secure and filled with love. They had experienced times of struggle, but there was never a struggle that they did not survive stronger and better than they were before.

She savored her good fortune and the blessings God had given her. She was happy that God intervened in her life, that she had turned to Him at the right time, and that He gave her the courage she needed to make the changes necessary to experience true happiness.

Janice learned to trust the biblical model of love she found in scripture. Her life with Martin had not been without trouble, but they had worked their way through disagreements and other hardships that periodically confronted them. Grounded with a proper perspective, mutual respect, and knowledge of how having these boundaries could keep them together, they were able to live together in peace and lasting love. She decided that she would write her story down so that other girls could read it and avoid the pitfalls that could entrap them.

Epilogue

God's love for us transcends any faults or flaws we possess. The Bible says, "While we were yet sinners, Christ died for us." Whenever we have done something wrong and need forgiveness, God is the one to whom we should run. In His word, there is always an answer to our dilemma. Our greatest challenge comes when we must own up to our part in what has happened. Once we have done this, we can move into accepting the perfect sacrifice that God provided for us.

If you have stumbled or made great mistakes like Janice, it doesn't matter if it is looking for love or any other failure; your answer for change is readily available. You only need to take the first step and turn to the one who provided your escape route before you ever failed.

Janice's story helps us to understand that we are not in control of our early circumstances. As children, we are subject to the direction of parents or guardians who, even though they may try hard, are not always able to shield us from hurt and other dangers. Sometimes they are at the core of our pain. Our early teachings and experiences can also create an obstructed view in our thinking. We are sometimes not aware of our intrinsic motivating factors. Her story also shows how we can overcome these challenges even after significant failures. The most crucial steps are to stop, turn to God, and ask for help.

Janice was fortunate to have in her background an early church experience that undergirded her. God sends us answers in many ways. The catalyst for you might be this book, a friend that invited you to church, or just a feeling that you need to change. The most important thing is to recognize where your hindered view or scotomas are and correct your thinking.

In our story, one of Janice's suppressed hurts resulted in an inability to recognize love. She later chose to use a biblical model to correct her definition of love. You have the same option to check your life and make the changes necessary to secure a sound future for yourself.

This story used fictional characters to teach real-life biblical principles. If you want to change your circumstances, the answer is as near to you as it was to Janice in our story. Stop, repent, and ask for help if you need it.

Jeremiah 17:14 (NIV)
[14] Heal me, LORD, and I will be healed;
Save me, and I will be saved,
for you are the one I praise.

THE ROAD TO REDEMPTION

BONUS GUIDE

Chapter 1
Values

Principle I: *We need God's transforming power to change our hearts so that our negative experiences do not affect our future decisions.*

We are born into circumstances that are not within the realm of our control. We do not get to choose our parents, other family members, or economic class. We usually love our parents or whoever had the privilege to guide us into adulthood, but imperfect people cannot create perfect lives for us. We live in a fallen world. Our development can sometimes leave us with emotions, habits, and behaviors that create blind spots in our lives. We can live unaware of the emotional walls we put up to protect ourselves or the pitfalls that lie before us. God created us in His image, so it is within our grasp to change and live into the new truth that He presents to us. When we replace the old information from our hurts and misinformation with the truth about who we are from God's perspective, we can live up to our true calling.

Janice became a teenager from a single-parent home, and as such, her memories of her family when they were together faded. She walked away from her childhood with the image of her handsome father, whom she adored but forgot how distant he was when he was there. Tucked away in her subconscious mind were her feelings of abandonment and dismay at his departure. It further disrupted her life when she lost her home and comfort zone. Life abruptly snatched her security and stability. The loss of her father was added to the loss of her familiar home, friends, and surroundings. Those changes demanded that she make mental adjustments to a new unwanted, unfamiliar life. Her sanity and happiness also demanded that she transcend her feelings of rejection, accept the new paradigm, and release the old one.

After her dad left, her escape from her disrupted family life was family TV shows. Reading and television seemed like the best way to find out about life, family, and love. The programs she watched had the power to transport her to more loving days when her life made sense. Her broken home life was now less than desirable; Janice was now adding, from television, an image of love that was empty and incomplete. Janice was praying for what she wanted, but she did not consider how her past would guide her current decisions and prayers. She failed to calculate how emotional scars, feelings of abandonment, and being unloved would influence her.

How about you? How much are your negative past experiences influencing your current decisions? Could it be that, like Janice, you need God's transforming power to help you replace negative influences from your past with new truth from his word about how valuable you are and how much he wants to be in a relationship with you?

Chapter Scripture: Galatians 4:2

² While they are children, they must obey those who are chosen to care for them. But when they reach the age the father set, they are free. Romans 12:2 NLT

Reflective Questions

1. Think about your life and list at least one wall you may have built to protect yourself that could cause you a problem now.

2. When there is no support for you at home, where can you effectively look for help?

3. What misconceptions about love can you get from modern media? Name three.

Prayer

Father, I bring all my past hurts and disappointments to you. Heal my wounded spirit. Help me to walk into all that you designed me to become.

Chapter 2
Jason

Principle II: *Believe what you see.*

Hindsight is always 20/20. Since we cannot see our futures to avoid the pitfalls that may be in our paths, we need the guidance of the Holy Spirit to help us manage ourselves better. We also need help with our concealed memories and the protective barriers built to keep out anything that could hurt us. Only then can we avoid some of our hindsight regrets.

At the beginning of their relationship, Jason was fun to have around. Janice decided to overlook his inconsiderate abusive behavior. When she saw him being mean to other people and making fun of them, she overlooked it. There was a need for Janice to believe what she saw. His actions did show her his real character. She needed to pay attention to the uneasy feeling she had when he did certain things. We have inner warning signals about things we need to pay attention to. Ignoring those inner warning signals can lead us to disaster. Making decisions based on her feelings for Jason was a mistake.

Janice spent the years after her father left burying her feelings and trying to bring normalcy back into her life. She dreamed about how she would repair her life when she was old enough to do so. She painstakingly mapped out the way that she believed was best for her. She would educate herself and become entirely sufficient to change her life. When she met Jason, she had no idea of the impact he would have on her spiritual life or the power he would have to change her entire future. His appeal to her had more to do with her impression of his background and privileges. She wanted what Jason had without any effort. She was more attracted to his life than to him.   She quickly abandoned her plan to follow him to take a shortcut to her new life. Moving into his apartment would afford her a more effortless experience than her plan did. His parents supplied everything, and she could partake of it. He said he would marry her, and in her heart, that would solidify her position in the world that she lost.

Janice prayed her way to the point where she had a solid path for a promising future, but her unfulfilled need for love and her desire to escape her home life derailed her. She had put up enough emotional walls to protect herself from hurtful memories so that even she was unaware of why she was willing to abandon her better judgment. All these elements set her up for Jason to convince her that she should choose love and deceit over sound judgment.

God is a redeemer and always has the power to turn our lives around once we seek Him for help. God always knows our future, where the wonderful places are, and the horrific pitfalls, as well. We always need His guiding hand to lead us forward in our lives.

Chapter Scripture: Proverbs 3:5-6

Trust the **LORD** *completely, and don't depend on your own knowledge. With every step you take, think about what He wants, and He will help you go the right way.*

Reflective Questions

1. List three problems living by emotions can cause.

2. Consider the relationships in your life that have obvious problems, but you overlook them. Should you be paying more attention to their effect on you?

3. Are the plans that you are making for your life based on emotion or sound evidence?

Prayer

Father, help me to remember your great love for me. You know all about my past and my future. Forgive me for not trusting you. Give me wisdom as I prepare to take hold of the future that you have prepared for me. Heavenly Father, I cast my cares on You because You care for me. Help me to trust you to guide me to sound decisions.

Chapter 3

Compromise

Principle III: *Love does not dishonor others.*

"Don't be fooled, bad friends will ruin good habits. Come back to your right way of thing and stop sinning." **1 Corinthians 15:33-34**

Janice had developed the awesome habit of praying as she designed her future and how she desired it to unfold. God had been her only ally as she grew up feeling lonely and unloved. It was his love that had embraced her when the pain of the loss of her former life had overwhelmed her. It was His grace that had flowed freely to her as she made school her place of refuge. How was Jason able to convince Janice to change herself so easily? If he really loved her, would he have disrupted her life to live a lie? Jason's motives were to satisfy himself, not Janice. True love does not draw you into situations that are bad for you. When you find yourself on this road, stop and rethink.

When you let someone into your life after you observe behavior by them that is contrary to the standard you hold for yourself, you are probably opening your life to a negative experience that you may well regret. Jason was kind to Janice but mean to other people. It flattered Janice when Jason paid attention to her because he was so popular and had an affluent lifestyle. His lifestyle, with its many possessions, a family life that offered him support and privileges, and the love of his parents, was in stark contrast to her life. After enough time with Jason, he became the voice in Janice's life to which she listened. She moved away from well-thought-out hard-earned success and plans. What voices are you listening to that can bring life-changing results to you?

Janice walked into, for all intents and purposes, a trap. Love does not dishonor. Love wants the best for you, not for itself, and it certainly does not lead you into a life of lies and disgrace. Janice felt strong emotions for Jason, and Jason felt strong emotions toward Janice. The difference between strong emotions and love is that love is not selfish or self-serving. We all need to understand how to manage strong emotions for someone and put them into proper perspective.

It is always important to be aware of the "traps" that are awaiting us. If you are unable to identify love, or if you are "desperately" looking for love, you can easily become a victim of your own making.

Feeling good about someone, enjoying their company, sexual attraction, affection, infatuation, nor lust is love. They may be a prelude to love, but these feelings will all fade. We could mistake any of these feelings for love. Jason was only thinking of himself and his wants and needs.

Chapter Scripture: 1 Corinthians 13:7-8

It always protects, always trusts, always hopes, always perseveres. Love never fails.

Reflective Questions

1. Is the need to be loved a strong motivation for you?

2. The scripture says that love protects. (1Cor.13 NIV) What does that mean to you?

3. Think about the situations and experiences that you may have suppressed that are affecting your behavior today and list at least two.

Prayer

Lord, I stand in faith and fully believe in your plan for my life. Thank you for your word that brings light and wisdom into my life. I recognize and affirm that the love that you describe in your word is steadfast and committed to the good of others. It is not selfish or self-serving. Help me to recognize love by using your word as a guide. Thank you for your leadership in every area of my life.

Chapter 4

Redemption

Courage to Move Forward

Principle IV: *When you know the truth, the truth makes you free.* (The truth allows you to advance with clarity)   **John 8:32**

At times you will find yourself at a crossroad moment when there are tough decisions to make; the power of knowing the truth can help you make the difficult decision that faces you. Don't avoid making the right decision because you fear the uncomfortable feeling it may give you. Trust God and do what is right; He will make your path straight.

"Today, I have given you a choice between life and death, success, and disaster.   **Deuteronomy 30:15.20**

Having courage does not mean that we are not afraid. On the contrary, having courage has more to do with our willingness to engage in challenges even when we are afraid or uncertain of the outcome. Courage is moving when I do not know how the outcome will affect me, and I do it anyway. When I conclude that I need to change, God's grace is there to supply the ability to make that change to align myself with His word. It is still my responsibility to make the necessary move. God's grace gives us both the desire and the ability to change. God's abundant grace is one of the truths that make us free.

Janice finds herself in a position where she can make a choice. The truth is that she had always been in the position to make this choice. At this point, as God's grace flows to her, the truth that "His strength is made perfect in weakness" takes center stage in her life. She concludes that she can accept her current situation as a victim, move in with one of her friends for the weekend and pray this blows over, or view this as an opportunity to change a situation where she is unhappy and unfulfilled. As a victim, she can stay confined to the dictations of her life with Jason and his infidelity, or she can move, with courage, to find a permanent solution that restores her dignity, inner purpose, and choices.

Janice had already yielded to temptation, violated her core moral code, lived a lie, and now finds that Jason is not faithful to all he promised her. In fact, after what she learned, he may not love her at all. As often happens when you allow your values to be compromised, the thing that she hoped was the ultimate answer for her life was crumbling to reveal its deception. She had to summon her inner faith to see a better life before her. What we do not realize sometimes is that we are one phone call away from freedom.

God is waiting for each of us to acknowledge our need for Him and His guidance. He only wants us to turn to Him so that He can rescue us from ourselves. Are there unavoidable consequences? Of course, but we do not have to face them alone. Even in the valley of the shadow of death, he is with us and comforts us. (Psalm 23)

Chapter Scripture: 1 Corinthians 10:13

The only temptations that you have are the same temptations that all people have. However, you can trust God. He will not let you be tempted more than you can bear. However, when you are tempted, God will also give you a way to escape that temptation. Then you will be able to endure it.

Reflective Questions

1. Are you willing to face the possibility of being uncomfortable to make changes to your life?

2. Are you willing to ask God for the grace to make life-affecting changes that can free you?

3. Could your hesitation to change be that you like things the way they are?

Prayer

Heavenly Father, you know all about me. You know my situation and my shortcomings. Give me the faith to proceed in the face of my fears. Bless me with the grace to overcome my challenges. Help me to remember that you, Lord, are always with me, and I am never alone. Thank you for helping me to overcome any moment of weakness that I may encounter.

Chapter 5

Rebound

Principle V: *We Can Rely on God's Love for Us*

The scripture declares: *"But if we confess our sins, God will forgive us. We can trust God to do this. He always does what is right. He will make us clean from all the wrong things we have done."*

1 John 1:9 (ERV)

God faithfully forgives us when we are in positions of failure and despair. His all-encompassing grace gives us what we do not deserve. When you decide to change any situation or bad habit, it is important that you cut ties with the people and situations that have the power to keep you tied to them. Sometimes it may require that you leave old friends and associates behind because when you are with them, they are not supportive of your desire to change. There are also places that you may find that you must stop frequenting. Holding on to them can impede your progress toward a better life.

It may be painful to make some of the breaks that you must make, but God promises that His grace is enough to see you through those moments. The thing that we must remember about God is that He will not pry us out of or away from anyone or anything. We must freely choose to walk away from our sins for Him to bless us. Some of the changes we need to make may not be a sin at all. They are habits and other impediments that will lead us down a path that is not best for us. When we make the decision and move towards changing our situation, we will then find the strength that He promises to give us to enable our decision.

First, Corinthians 15:33 tells us that evil communications corrupt good manners. As Janice allowed Jason to become her sole confidant and advisor, he was able to use her weaknesses to his advantage. What voices are you listening to that can bring life-changing results to you?

Janice stepped into a snare when she stopped trusting God and started trusting Jason. His promises and affection appealed to a desperate need within her to be significant to someone.

Janice ignored her feeling of loss when she traded one bad situation for another. There were warnings within her that she overrode. Her temptation to have a quick route to success was overwhelming her good judgment, which up to now had sustained her. Jason painted a picture of a shortcut to the life and love that she was desperate to experience. His would eliminate a lot of the hard work and sacrifice that her plans would demand. It offered the illusion of an easy road to the future she desired. If she had measured what he offered to a biblical definition of love, she would see the purely selfish motive behind his empty requests.

It is always important to be aware of the "counterfeits" offered to us. If it seems too good to be true, don't be afraid to test it. When it is a real blessing, it will stand the test without failing.

Feeling good about someone, enjoying their company, sexual attraction, affection, infatuation, nor lust is love. They may be a precursor to romantic love and could be mistaken for love, but those feelings are unstable and tend to fade with time. The love that God has for us to experience is stable and not apt to violate our covenant with Him. Jason, in his effort to satisfy himself, his wants, and his needs, disallowed what she wanted as unimportant. If he truly loved her, his efforts would have been to help her succeed in following her vision for herself so that she would be fulfilled.

One of the results of Jesus' death is that in moments of profound failure, we can make our way back to God. In these critical times, when our emotions are raw, and we feel ashamed and disconnected from God, He is closer than we can imagine Him to be. In these dark moments, when we realize that we have failed in our portion of our relationship with God, it is then that He is closest to us. We tend to hide from Him, as Adam and Eve hid in the garden. But the scripture tells us to *"Come boldly to the throne of grace that we might obtain mercy and find grace in the time of need."* **Hebrew 4:16** These are the times that we should cling to our Savior so that He can enable us with the courage to rebound from our failure.

Chapter Scripture: 2 Corinthians 5:17 (TLB)

[17] When someone becomes a Christian, he becomes a brand-new person inside. He is not the same anymore. A new life has begun!

Reflective Questions

1. How do you define love?

2. How can you differentiate between lust and love?

3. Why should we closely examine shortcuts offered to us as we move through life?

Prayer

Father, thank you for Your love for me and Your willingness to forgive.

Renewal

Principle VI: *His Mercy is Everlasting* **Psalm 100:5**

*Because of the **LORD**'s great love, we are not consumed, for his compassions never fail. They are new every morning…*

Lamentations 3:21-23

Every morning we open our eyes; God's love and compassion are there to usher us into our new day. He alone loves us unconditionally and is willing to forgive our wrongs. It is incumbent upon us to repent and accept His great gift. We do not have to carry around our guilt and shame. He forgives, and we must only accept His forgiveness.

A new start can be challenging. There may be times when you have to ignore those who will not forgive you or transcend any negative vibes you feel to become your ultimate best version of yourself. You must learn not to base your decisions on emotions but let biblically sound principles guide you to a better place. Because emotions are changeable and not always dependable, the word of God holds the keys to the principles on which you can base choices that govern your future. A seasoned Godly advisor will also help you in these times.

Janice made a courageous change in her life. She decided to leave Jason for good and not just for the weekend. In doing that, she took control of her future and the changes she needed to make to be free. That declaration itself was the first step to her new life. No doubt, the decision to leave Jason was painful and distressing. She had to be willing to allow herself to feel those things she needed to disconnect from so that she could start anew. She truly loved Jason, but her love alone could not overcome all the frustration living a lie had caused her.

It was vital that she removed herself from the source of her problem. There was no way to stay with Jason and make critically necessary adjustments to her life. He was perfectly willing to destroy any aspiration she had for herself to satisfy his desires. The conversion she needed to make required her to sever ties to her relationship with Jason. She must remove herself from his reach and chart a better path for her life. Trying to hold on to Jason and change would have tainted that start. He would keep her emotions and her decisions clouded as he had before.

When you need to make a new start, dragging old problems and debris with you will delay and, perhaps even abort, your fresh start.

Chapter Scripture —Luke 5:36-38 (NASB)

36 Jesus told them this story: "No one takes the cloth off a new coat to cover a hole in an old coat. That would ruin the new coat, and the cloth from the new coat would not be the same as the old cloth. 37 Also, no one ever pours new wine into old wineskins. The new wine would break them. The wine would spill out, and the wineskins would be ruined. 38 You always put new wine into new wineskins.

Reflective Questions

1. Why is it important not to carry old questionable habits on your new journey?

2. How willing are you to sacrifice to gain your new start?

3. Are your emotions holding you captive to a situation that you need to leave?

Prayer

Lord, as I begin anew with Christ, help me to re-establish my life with all things new, new ways to relate to friends, new places to go, and new things to do.

Chapter 7

Restoration

Principle VIII: *God Restores*

"I will restore to you the years the locusts have eaten... **Joel 2:25**

Just when you believe that your ambitions for yourself are lost or that you have blown that perfect opportunity, God can restore what you think you have lost. So, when your fear of making a change in your life hinges on the idea that you will lose so much that you will never regain it, TRUST GOD. He restores, and it is usually better than what you had before.

God's plan for us is to give us hope and a future; His will for us is to prosper and be in health even as our soul prospers. He offers us peace during our storms and promises to be with us always. Janice moved from disgrace to grace by accepting God's promises for her life. She still had to make the necessary changes to allow refreshing of her mind. After making those sacrifices, she was now able to live in the good days of life, fulfill her dreams, and through hard work, make a new start.

While mercy is withholding some penalty that you do deserve, grace is the undeserved favor that gives you a gift that you do not merit. God's grace was with Janice, but how much of this could she have avoided if she had just talked it over with an older, trusted person whose experience and wisdom could have helped her? It could have been that she did not seek out another opinion because she believed she did not have an ally in her fight to change her life into something better. But it could have been that she did not seek counsel when she changed her decision because she knew deep inside that this change was not in her best interest and could very possibly fail. She knew that this was a risky venture and that she would be advised not to make life changes that were not her idea at all based on emotional attachments. In her innermost being, she wanted to believe the lie.

A shortcut to happiness is so much more appealing than a plan that takes hard work and sacrifice to achieve. Shortcuts can be dangerous because they eliminate a portion of the journey and remove some of the necessary encounters that will make your life fuller and complete. When you are in the process of making a decision that can have life-affecting consequences, find someone to talk to, seasoned in the spirit, who will not tell you what you want to hear but give you sound advice. If you don't know any, find one.

Even when you do take the shortcut and lose your way, God, the restorer, can reestablish your life. All He needs is for you to acknowledge your mistake and your need for Him.

Chapter Scripture - 1 Peter 5:10 (ERV)

[10] Yes, you will suffer for a short time. But after that, God will make everything right. He will make you strong. He will support you and keep you from falling. He is the God who gives all grace. He chose you to share in his glory in Christ. That glory will continue forever.

Reflective Questions

1. Why is it so tempting to take the shortcut after taking the time to figure out a situation and count up the cost?

2. What advice would you have given Janice if she confided her situation to you?

3. Are you in a situation that could get better if you seek advice from a more experienced person?

Prayer

Father, as I boldly approach the throne of grace, lead me to the paths in life that are your will for me. Help me to know when it is best to seek counsel and not depend on my understanding. Father, put wise counselors in my path and grant me the grace to listen and know when You are directing me.

Chapter 8

Breadcrumbs

Principle VII: *Old Habits Always Return to Try Your Resolve*

The Grimm Brothers wrote a tale called Hansel and Gretel. In the story, two children, a brother, and sister, lived with their father and stepmother. Their stepmother, wanting to rid herself of them, plotted to take them far into the forest and leave them. She decided to take them so deep into the forest that they could not find their way home. She intended to rid herself of them forever. However, overhearing her plan, they loaded their pockets first with rocks, then with breadcrumbs, and left a trail behind them as she took them deeper and deeper into the woods. After she left them in the woods, they planned to use the trail they had left to find their way home.

Janice had left Jason's apartment, supposedly left the relationship, and left the city and state where they lived together, but she kept her phone number, one that Jason knew so well. Like Hansel and Gretel, Janice left a trail for Jason to find her. On the surface, she had gone to great lengths to cut all ties with Jason, yet she kept one way for him to find her. In her heart, she had not been willing to let go completely. Eventually, Jason would find his way to her with the trail she had left for him to follow. Only then did she realize that her own heart had deceived her; she left a door open for him to return. She needed to know that he cared and that she was not so dispensable; even after his infidelity, she longed to feel that he loved her and had just made a terrible mistake. Then she would not feel like such a fool. His finding her would somehow validate the fact that her decision to believe in her happily ever after with him had not been a lie from the very beginning.

It is almost a certainty that when you leave some habit or person behind you, that the temptation to return to it will present itself. Sometimes it happens when you least expect it. Many times, it is when trouble or loneliness appears in your life. Whatever the reason, you can almost guarantee that what you left behind will resurface to try your resolve. Do you mean what you have declared? It is in those moments that if you ask Him, God will pour out his grace to help you resist the temptation. Keep your eyes forward and trust your decision to leave whatever it is behind. Is there anything in your life that you are trying to break away from but have left just one door open for its return? Have you left one breadcrumb trail behind you? Be careful not to hold on to some small part of your past when you attempt to break away from something. If you consider the possibilities too long, the urge will grow, and you will find yourself ensnared again.

Chapter Scripture   Romans 12:2 (MSG)
Put your Life into Gods hands.

So, here's what I want you to do, God helping you: Take your everyday, ordinary life—your sleeping, eating, going to work, and walking-around life and place it before God as an offering. Embracing what God does for you is the best thing you can do for him. Don't become so well-adjusted to your culture that you fit into it without even thinking. Instead, fix your attention on God. You'll be changed from the inside out. Readily recognize what he wants from you, and quickly respond to it. Unlike the culture around you, always dragging you down to its level of immaturity, God brings the best out of you and develops well-formed maturity in you.

Reflective Questions

1. If a relationship has soured, do you think you can shock the person into changing their mind?

2. If they do change their minds, can shocking them change their character? Why, why not?

3. Are you honest with yourself about the relationships in your life?

Prayer

Father, as I pursue a better way of life, I acknowledge that you are the God who knows my tomorrow. I seek the path that you have laid for me and deny any other distractions and hindrances that come my way.

Chapter 9

The Wedding

Principle IX: *God's Love for Us Never Fails*

*Delight thyself also in the **LORD**: and he shall give thee the desires of thine heart. Commit thy way unto the **LORD**; trust also in him, and he shall bring it to pass.* **Psalm 37:4-5 (KJV)**

Janice longed for love, and God brought love to her. The love God brought her, however, was one that was not self-serving and one that would not fail her. He alone knows our end from our beginning, and He can see where our choices will lead. Trust the principles in the word or trust wise advice even when it goes against emotional wants.

Janice started her journey with meticulous planning and a lot of hope. Then, a series of mistakes caused her to go off-track. The errors in judgment that Janice made could mostly be traced back to listening to the wrong voice. But the Bible plainly tells us that our own lusts and desires draw us away. Along with her meticulous plans was a desire to have her need for love fulfilled right away. We must monitor our inner desires lest a fake promise will lure us from our safe place. However, once Janice confronted the truth about her situation, coupled with her despair and disappointment, she did not wallow in her despair but got herself up and moved forward. She turned to God in her distress and walked away from her mistake.

Janice accepted God's forgiveness and cut ties with her past. She confessed to her mother that she misled her and her past mistake to Martin, with whom she would share her life. She worked hard and got the degree that was her heart's desire and was able to be free to live the life she so desperately desired.

Do not delay if your life is out of control. Take the necessary steps, like Janice, to make essential changes so you can start over with a clean slate.

Chapter Scripture - Isaiah 58:8

If you do these things, your light will begin to shine like the light of dawn. Then your wounds will heal. Your "Goodness" will walk in front of you, and the Glory of the LORD will come following behind you.

Reflective Questions

1. If God never fails, why do these things happen to us?

2. How should you handle the embarrassment when you fail?

3. Do you believe that you are beyond God's reach?

Prayer

Father, I pray for your restoring grace. I declare that as I begin my life anew with you. I will experience a restoration in my life that will bring me joy and peace.

Elder Beverly Davis

Visit the Author's blog "Consider This Monthly Devotional" at ministerbev.com

ABOUT THE AUTHOR

Beverly Davis has a passion for God's people. Ordained in 1981, she ministers to those whose lives are in crisis. Beverly is an educator and an inspirational speaker. She holds a bachelor's degree in Business Administration, a master's degrees in both Business Administration and Adult Education and Community Leadership.

Made in the USA
Columbia, SC
14 February 2024

31451233R00109